GUILLOTINE
Bride

I'm just a dragon girl who'll destroy the world.

T0017459

Ragnarok:

≪DRAGON≫ Factor

"I'm! Going to! Save you!"

"...I am now this planet's apex predator."

HIGH SCHOOL STUDENT
Ryuunosuke Dazai

DRAGON GIRL
Rinne Irako

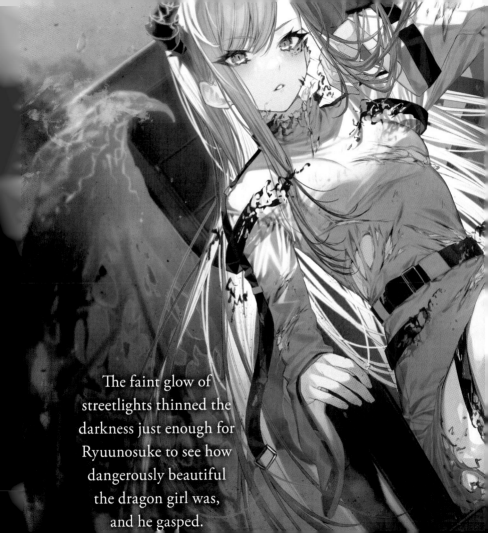

The faint glow of
streetlights thinned the
darkness just enough for
Ryuunosuke to see how
dangerously beautiful
the dragon girl was,
and he gasped.

"How many years has it been since my last descent…?"

The girl leaned back and crossed her legs, eyeing Ryuunosuke haughtily. She made the plain chair look like a throne.

GUILLOTINE Bride

I'm just a dragon girl who'll destroy the world.

Daigo Murasaki

Illustration by

Kayahara

YEN ON
NEW YORK

GUILLOTINE Bride

Daigo Murasaki

Translation by Kiki Piatkowska
Cover art by Kayahara

DANTODAI NO HANAYOME Vol. 1 SEKAI O HOROBOSU FUTSUTSUKANA WATASHI DESUGA
©Daigo Murasaki, Kayahara 2022
First published in Japan in 2022 by KADOKAWA CORPORATION, Tokyo. English translation rights arranged with KADOKAWA CORPORATION, Tokyo through TUTTLE-MORI AGENCY, INC., Tokyo.

English translation © 2024 by Yen Press, LLC

Yen On
150 West 30th Street, 19th Floor
New York, NY 10001

Visit us at yenpress.com ◆ facebook.com/yenpress ◆ twitter.com/yenpress
yenpress.tumblr.com ◆ instagram.com/yenpress

First Yen On Edition: May 2024
Edited by Yen On Editorial: Leilah Labossiere
Designed by Yen Press Design: Liz Parlett

Yen On is an imprint of Yen Press, LLC.
The Yen On name and logo are trademarks of Yen Press, LLC.

Library of Congress Cataloging-in-Publication Data
Names: Murasaki, Daigo, author. | Kayahara, illustrator. | Piatkowska,
    Kiki, translator.
Title: Guillotine bride / Daigo Murasaki ; illustration by Kayahara ;
    translation by Kiki Piatkowska.
Other titles: Dantoudai no hanayome. English
Description: First Yen On edition. | New York, NY : Yen On, 2024- |
Identifiers: LCCN 2023057805 | ISBN 9781975392390 (trade paperback)
Subjects: CYAC: Fantasy. | Marriage—Fiction. | LCGFT: Fantasy fiction. |
    Action and adventure fiction. | Light novels.
Classification: LCC PZ7.1.M837 Gu 2024 | DDC [Fic]—dc23
LC record available at https://lccn.loc.gov/2023057805

ISBNs: 978-1-9753-9239-0 (paperback)
       978-1-9753-9240-6 (ebook)

10 9 8 7 6 5 4 3 2 1

LSC-C

Printed in the United States of America

PROLOGUE

The Cradle of Guillotinism

"Subject FF03-100, Rinne Irako, is hereby sentenced to death."

The sentence was spoken quietly, with a businesslike lack of emotion. The courtroom was large and sterile. The ghostly holograms of seven judges glowed in the semidarkness, staring down at the accused from their high seats. The atmosphere would be more suited to a meeting of some evil organization or a secret society rather than a court hearing.

"This is a decision issued by the state," one of the hologram men said gravely.

It wasn't a fair trial. The prosecutor was absent. The defendant didn't have an attorney. Other than the seven judges and the defendant, there was only one more person present—a spectator. No one could raise objections or ask to cross-examine any witnesses. The judges announced their verdict, and that was it.

This hearing gave the judiciaries absolute power, which violated the separation of powers in the Japanese constitution, but this particular case was beyond the judicial process. The sentence could not be appealed.

" ... "

The defendant, confined in a transparent prison cell at the center of the courtroom, was silent. She didn't show any sign of defiance. But she probably *couldn't*. The temperature in that miniature prison was −60°C. No human could survive such extreme cold, yet the defendant was still alive. Based on this, it could be inferred that she was not human. However, that was already apparent due to...*certain parts of her anatomy.*

The defendant, sealed in that icy prison, wasn't even allowed to hear her sentence.

The girl looked as if she was in her midteens. At that age, she shouldn't even have been tried in court; she'd be protected by Japanese law as a minor.

She had long, beautiful hair and a pretty face. In her piercingly cold cell, she was like an impossibly perfect ice sculpture.

They had put her in a straitjacket, which was fastened with multiple belts, depriving her of both freedom and dignity. In that frigid jail cell, the girl was robbed of all but her beauty, which nothing could diminish.

The girl did look quite human, but she was, in fact, a dragon.

"Please hold off on the execution!" shouted the lone spectator, a girl in a white lab coat. "Give me just a little more time—that's all I'm asking for!"

The spectator's plea sounded as desperate as if she was a proxy of the silenced dragon girl.

The holographic men were unmoved.

"It was none other than you, Akeda, who recorded an analysis of her destructive potential when out of control."

"You are correct."

"And you have concluded that she has the ability to destroy the twenty largest nations in the world. From our point of view, the erasure of modern civilizations equals the erasure of humanity."

"That certainly is a valid interpretation, but—"

"We fully understand the subject is a precious resource we could possibly use to our advantage, and we admit that our decision dishonorably violates human rights. Indeed, destroying this resource will put us, the Calamity Research Institute, at a disadvantage against the Order," the hologram continued. "However, the risk to humanity outweighs the potential gains. We have a duty to protect our species, even if it means extinguishing the life of this young person."

"..."

The girl in the lab coat fell silent, unable to argue with the Special Calamity Prevention Research Institute's reasoning, even as her heart screamed that it wasn't right.

"If only there was some miraculous method of preventing this danger...," another one of the hologram men remarked offhandedly.

"A miraculous method...," the girl in the lab coat repeated, thinking. "If we found someone with a Sacred Sealing Ring, for example?"

Her suggestion was met with laughter.

"A Sacred Sealing Ring? You'd have an easier time finding a needle in a haystack. A miracle like that simply isn't going to happen. You should be smart enough not to cling to such foolish hopes."

The girl said nothing.

"Are there no further objections?" one of the judges asked, knowing full well that there wouldn't be any.

"The execution will be carried out by guillotine in twenty-four hours."

The courtroom was silent for a few moments.

"By guillotine?" one of the hologram men asked with distaste. "It horrifies me to think of executing a young lady in such a way."

"It may be customary, but *guillotine* has an unnecessarily cruel ring to it, doesn't it?"

"Your concerns are misplaced. An execution is an execution."

Even though some of the judges pitied the dragon girl, nothing could be done to change the sentence.

"This court session is over. You may leave."

The ghostly holograms of the judges vanished, leaving only the two girls in the room. The girl in the lab coat crumpled to her knees. She placed her hands on the dragon girl's icy cell, which emitted a faint blue glow.

"I'm sorry." The girl's voice was tinged with regret. "I'm sorry, Rinne. I couldn't save you..."

The dragon girl couldn't hear her voice, but she felt the vibrations of footsteps as she was carried to the guillotine.

CHAPTER 1

Close Encounter of the Third Kind

He was having a bizarre dream.

"Help as many people as you can, for the both of us."

Those words would be his curse.

"Promise me that."

The dragon girl died amid fierce flames. Maybe he could've saved her, if only he wasn't so weak. The guilt clung to him like dirt that wouldn't wash off no matter how much he scrubbed. Light flickered faintly on his left hand, like a flame—a keepsake from her.

Until her death, the dragon girl had protected both him and the phoenix, but now the flames rose, mercilessly trying to claim two lives.

The air became thick as tar, and the boy struggled to breathe, but the glare of fury in his eyes remained as painfully bright as the midsummer sun at its zenith. He wanted to yell, but his throat and his lungs were scorched. He wanted to escape, but his right arm wouldn't move, and he couldn't feel his legs at all. Silently screaming, he watched the flames consume the dragon girl.

"You won't be able to fulfill your promise to her if you die. It mustn't happen," whispered the phoenix, whose life the dragon had been protecting.

The boy's consciousness was fading, but he managed to extend his left arm toward her, and the burning sensation in his ring finger momentarily flared up. Even as the raging flames painted everything around him crimson, the light radiating from his ring finger shone through. It, too, rose like a flame, burning his finger.

"That's why...we must ■ ■*."*

He cursed the phoenix for what she had done to his left hand.

◆

The boy woke from his dream.

"Ngh... Must've nodded off..."

He wiped drool from the corner of his mouth with his hand. As always, he'd already forgotten what the dream was about, but he was certain it was the same recurring dream he usually had.

The boy was in the student council room. He had long bangs, sharp eyes, and lines on his cheek—an impression of the arm he'd slept on. He was sitting in a folding chair, hunched over a table.

"The president's not here yet. Guess I have some time."

He checked the time on his outdated smartphone, stretched, and stood from his chair to get ready.

There were probably quite a few students at West Kokonoe Metropolitan High School who couldn't put the name to the face of most student council members. Many didn't care who got elected to the council, and there was a fair number who didn't even know the name of the student council president.

"Looking good. Definitely getting bigger..."

But while students might draw a blank when asked who the student council president was, not a single one could forget the name of the vice president—this boy.

"Yeah, that's it... Great..."

It was May, one month since the start of the new school year, and everybody already knew this particular second-year student.

"It's shaping up nicely..."

Suddenly, the door flew open, and a girl with long golden pigtails strode in.

"Good day, student council! Are you moping in your little room as usual? Count yourself lucky! The most beautiful girl in the world is here!" she said in a charming, clear voice.

At the center of the room was a long table piled high with paperwork. Folding chairs were arranged around it. A steel shelving unit by the wall was lined with folders. On the wall opposite the door was a whiteboard with a schedule written in blue marker.

A white shirt, necktie, and a blazer were hung over the back of one of the folding chairs. Their owner was standing in front of a mirror at the far end of the room. He was none other than...

"Ryuunosuke Dazai! What are you doing...?"

The girl saw bulging deltoid muscles, well-defined pectorals, tight obliques, and an immaculate six-pack. Ryuunosuke had been posing in front of the mirror, unabashedly exposed from the waist up.

"Eeeeeep!"

"Why are *you* screaming? If anyone should be screaming in shock, that should be me, don't you think?!" the girl scolded him, confused by Ryuunosuke shrieking like an embarrassed damsel—albeit in a low, manly voice.

"Er, I guess you've got a point there," he conceded. "Anyway, Abara, when will you learn to knock first?"

"You're calling me Abara again? When will you learn to call me Marie?"

"Maybe when you stop calling me by my full name, Aide-to-the-Student-Council's-Vice-President Mari Vlad Abara!"

"I only do that because you won't call me Marie. Use that name for me, and I'll do aaanything you ask."

"Over my dead body. Your name's too silly."

"Says Ryuunosuke Dazai, with a name that belongs on the spine of a cobweb-covered literary classic no one wants to read!"

Mari pouted peevishly, closing the door behind her without looking. She brushed her sparkling golden hair away from her face. Like Ryuunosuke, she was a member of the student council. She was one year his junior. Her beauty was so off the charts that even calling her the most beautiful girl in the world didn't seem to do her justice. Her unbelievably bright eyes caught the last rays of the springtime sun, glinting like emeralds. Her face was chiseled more finely than an exquisite diamond. Her beauty was a rare treasure that attracted many.

She was dressed casually in a uniform blazer and a short skirt that accentuated her long legs, with a choker around her neck. She dazzled onlookers just by walking into a room. At the moment, though, it was the half-naked boy who drew more attention.

Mari put down her bag on the long table. A pink bunny-like mascot character key ring that was hooked to the bag jingled.

"So anyway, what are you doing here, stripped down to the waist?" She sat down on one of the folding chairs.

"Can't tell? I'm checking out my musculature, obviously."

Ryuunosuke went to pick up his shirt from the chair it was hanging on.

"Er…what? Why would you be doing that here? Don't make it sound like it's normal."

"It's as normal as you checking your makeup or seeing if you've got nose hairs sticking out."

"I guess I do check my makeup throughout the day… But nose hairs?! A pretty girl like me doesn't have nose hair! And you can't compare what you were doing here to touching up makeup! …You do have a nicer body than I expected, though."

"Think about it this way: It's good to have a muscular guy around in case a bear attacks a frail young girl like you, Abara."

"No matter how much you lift, a human can't overpower a *bear*! I could defeat one with my little finger, of course. But why are you preparing for bear attacks?"

"We get bears in these parts, you know."

"In Tokyo? Come on."

Mari watched as Ryuunosuke put his shirt back on.

"You're hiding a nice bod under those clothes, but you don't do any sports, do you?"

"Hmm? Nah. I get called to help out sometimes, but it's nothing regular. I'm not in any clubs, but I do something even more manly—martial arts. To be more precise, karate. Remotely."

Ryuunosuke stood on one leg and struck a pose.

"Isn't that a kung fu stance? And you said you're learning karate... remotely? Aren't you the least bit embarrassed to admit that?"

Everyone who knew Ryuunosuke Dazai would agree that he was a weirdo. Whether the rumors about him—such as he caught a purse-snatcher, saved a student harassed by delinquents from another school, threw a bully into the swimming pool and ended their wrongdoing once and for all—were true or embellished by overactive imaginations, the fact that there were so many rumors of this sort was proof that he was not an ordinary student. Before long, he'd been nicknamed the Dragon of West Kokonoe, and it had stuck. Ryuunosuke personally thought it sounded dumb and wished people would stop calling him that.

"Why are you learning karate remotely?"

"Because I wanted to learn a martial art but don't have time to go to a gym. Luckily, I can just do it online!"

Mari sighed.

"Why did I have to fall for this idiot...?" she muttered under her breath.

"Hmm? What was that?"

"Nothing. Say, Ryuunosuke Dazai, won't you go with me to Saburou's next time I'm free?"

"Um... I don't know..."

"Come on, please say yes to a balanced meal of delicious fatty, garlic pork with vegetables!"

Mari walked closer to Ryuunosuke, who kept backing up until he was in the corner. Mari grabbed his arm.

"H-hey, what are you doing? Let go!"

"Normally, you play it cool, but this is affecting you, isn't it? Your face is all red. I'm starting to enjoy this."

Mari grinned at him devilishly.

"Enough! A-Abara, behave!"

"Heh-heh… Why don't you use the karate skills you learned online to free yourself from me?"

Mari reached for the top button of Ryuunosuke's shirt…

"N-no, STOP!"

Suddenly, the door opened. Two girls took in the scene in the room.

"Dazai boy and Abara. What are you doing?"

"Y-you can't do such things in the student council room! Ryuu, Mari, please don't be indecent!"

One of the newcomers was a girl so petite, she could be mistaken for an elementary schooler, but something about her mannerism betrayed her fierce intelligence.

The other girl seemed timid. She had covered her eyes with her hands and was peeking at Ryuunosuke and Mari from between her fingers.

"I-Isurugi…! President…!"

The timid girl was Aya Isurugi, a second-year student acting as the student council's secretary. The small girl was Ranko Akeda, the student council president. She was a third-year.

"Oh no! My secret romance with Ryuunosuke Dazai has come to light!"

"Don't play dumb, Abara! Everyone can see you're just forcing yourself onto me!"

"I thought you were the straitlaced type," Aya said to Ryuunosuke. "This is very improper."

"We should be model students. Your shameless flirting could have a detrimental effect on the student body's morale, and as the student council president, I'll be held responsible. Wait until you're off school grounds to get frisky!"

"R-Ranko, don't encourage PDA outside the school gates," Aya scolded.

"No, please listen! You're jumping to the wrong conclusions, although I can totally see why you'd do that after coming in and seeing

us like this… I swear, I was checking out my upper body shirtless when Mari walked in on me and—"

"He admits to being shirtless in front of me!" Mari declared.

"You were naked in the student council room, Ryuu…?"

"See, Dazai boy? Even your childhood friend Aya is mortified by your perversion."

"Oh, no, no," Aya reassured the president. "I was just thinking that there's no need for him to strip in the student council room to look at his muscles. He already does that every morning before leaving his house…"

"Ah, I see what you're doing! Asserting your dominance as his close friend by letting us all know you live close and walk to school with him!" Mari shouted.

"What? No, I didn't mean it like that!"

Ranko, still in the doorway, shot Ryuunosuke a frosty look.

"So I gather Dazai boy lets out his inner pervert no matter where he is, whether at school or at home."

"No! I'm not a perv! I had my pants on the whole time!"

"Even baring the upper body is not something you should be doing in this room, Dazai boy."

"Anyone other than Mari would've been grossed out to find you like that," Aya added.

"Ryuunosuke Dazai, I don't mind if you're gross. I'll love you all the same," Mari said affectionately.

"I don't want it! Are you ever going to let go of me, Abara?!"

"Okay, okay."

Mari stopped clutching his clothes and moved away from him.

"How unfortunate that Aya and the President have arrived, bringing our fun to a premature end. We'll have to pick up where we left off later."

"No, there won't be any more of this!"

Confrontations like this had become a daily occurrence since Mari joined the student council. Ranko and Aya made their way to their chairs and sat down for the meeting, quite used to the others' antics. Ranko sat at the head of the table on the far end of the room. Aya, the secretary, sat on the right side of the table, with Ryuunosuke the vice president and his assistant, Mari, on the left side. They took out notebooks and laptops and got to work.

"Isurugi, do you know what's happened to our treasurer?" Ryuunosuke asked, rubbing the base of his ring finger with the index finger of his other hand—an unconscious habit of his.

"Owari hasn't told me anything. Maybe he's sick again?"

"I guess. He's always been sick a lot. We'll have to make do without him."

Ranko walked over to the shelves and pulled out a folder. She turned to Ryuunosuke.

"Dazai boy, I have a question."

It was her custom to refer to Ryuunosuke as "Dazai boy" even though she was only one year his senior and looked like an elementary schooler to boot. Ryuunosuke didn't really like it, but he figured that it was her way of keeping him at a comfortable distance.

"Sure, shoot."

"I can't find the Nature Appreciation Festival folder here. Why is that?"

"Ah, that project's complete. I was going to report to you about it later."

"But we need approval from the ward office and Professor Tazumi…"

"I went ahead and sorted it out already."

"Well, having a proactive subordinate like you makes my life easier. Getting you this job was the best decision I made. Cost me only ten canteen vouchers. You take care of all the tedious tasks."

"I'm glad you helped me get on the council. I'm happy to be your drudge."

"P-President! Doesn't that violate the student council election regulations…?"

Ranko shot Aya a smug look.

"I assure you I haven't done anything specifically forbidden by the regulations…"

Then she yawned widely.

"Yawning during our meeting…?"

While it was normal for Ranko to seem low-energy, she looked oddly tired that day. She even had dark bags under her eyes.

"Oh, excuse me. Things have been a little hectic for me lately."

"Hello? I have something *actually* important to bring up," said Mari. She alone had nothing assigned to her and was half sprawled on the table.

"I'm supposed to be the vice president's assistant, but I have no work to do at all. He does everything by himself, leaving zero for me!"

"If he can handle everything without help, then of course there's nothing left for you. By the way, Dazai boy, mind finishing up Owari's work as well? It's been piling up. I've got someplace to be today, so I can't stay long. Also, it's too tedious."

"That last one's the more important reason, huh…"

"Hmph," Mari huffed, eyeing Ranko.

"Sure. I'll take care of it."

"What? Ryuunosuke Dazai does anything if you just ask him? Aya, has he always been like this?" Mari asked.

"Well… He helps out even *without* being asked…"

"Why bother, Ryuunosuke Dazai?"

"It's no bother. If there's something I'm able to do for others, I just do it. Makes sense to me."

"Doesn't make sense to me, though," Mari said with a pout.

"Then why don't you help him with Owari's work, Abara?" asked Ranko. "You can use this room late into the evening. I'll let the teachers know you'll be here."

"No way! I have a life after school, you know!" Mari protested.

"You have a part-time job or something?"

"Something like that, yes. Girls have many secrets," she said vaguely, then slammed both her hands on the table. "All I wanted to say is, you're sacrificing yourself too much for others, Ryuunosuke Dazai! You go out of your way to help people even when they don't deserve it."

"I see it as him having a virtuous character," said Ranko. "Although, he does go overboard, like when he lent money to another student despite being broke. He even got a job to have money to lend to people in need…"

"I'd just like him to…rely on me for a change sometimes. Eh, whatever…"

"I never asked for your opinion on my way of life!" Ryuunosuke shouted. "I just… It's like a—a hobby for me! Helping people is my hobby. I find people who need assistance, lend them a hand, and that makes me feel good. I volunteer and I work on the side, and everyone fusses over me for being an upstanding citizen. I just like it."

"Same defense as always," Mari said, poking his face with one finger. "If you keep getting involved in other people's trouble, one day, you'll find yourself in way over your head."

◆

Night had fallen over Kokonoe City. A helicopter flew in from the west. With dark camouflage and its anti-collision lights off, it blended into the night sky. It was unlikely that anyone would spot it from the ground.

The helicopter carried five people. A girl in a white lab coat sat opposite from two guards armed with automatic rifles. Even though they were in peaceful Japan, the atmosphere in the helicopter was as tense as if they were in the middle of a war zone.

The guards were military personnel who'd been selected from the elite soldiers trained to combat terrorists. The reason such specialists were needed was on board with them in the cargo hatch.

A small container fastened with several belts was in that hatch. Its contents set everyone on edge, making the aircraft feel cramped.

The youngest of the armed men couldn't stand the tense silence any longer.

"You'd think we were transporting a lion, with all these safety measures," he joked, glancing at the container.

"Your first time, Kuroi?" asked an older, bigger man.

"Yeah. You do this all the time, Yanagida?"

"Can't say I do. Would be a relaxing trip if we were transporting a lion. It wouldn't survive a shot from this."

The man lifted his rifle.

"What, our cargo can't be killed with a gun?"

"...You didn't read the brief, did you?"

"No, no! Of course I did. Skimmed it at least. But it seemed too exaggerated..."

"Can't blame you for finding it hard to believe. But let me tell you, two generations ago when they had to deal with the dragon girl in America, they had to bring out tanks and fighter aircrafts."

"You can't be serious."

"I am. And now get this: Our cargo's dragon factor is far stronger than that one's. All hell would break loose if she went out of control. Not to worry, though—she's weakened and sedated."

"This mythical girl's a real monster, huh?"

"That's a very unkind thing to say," the third passenger, the girl in the white lab coat, interrupted. She'd been listening to the men's conversation through her headset. "She's going to be killed for what she is. A teenage girl is going to be put to death. How can you call her a monster?" She looked toward the container with pity in her eyes. "You should feel sorry for her."

◆

Inside the container was Rinne Irako, sitting in a chair with the straitjacket on. The temperature inside the container, which was made from tungsten, was −60°C. A dragon factor suppressant was being delivered to her body via several tubes running into her back from a machine behind the chair.

A human wouldn't be able to survive under those conditions. But then again, nobody would even think of doing this to a human. The power she possessed was clearly feared to a ridiculous extent.

"This mythical girl's a real monster, huh?"

"..."

Irako's ears twitched. Despite the extreme conditions in the container, she was alive, and although she was immobilized, her senses worked just fine. She heard what the others were saying despite the thick walls of the container and the deafening background noise of the helicopter's rotor. Because her senses were sharper than normal for a human, she was the first to notice that something had changed.

"...!"

She wanted to call out a warning, but she couldn't. The next instant, lightning struck the helicopter with a bluish flash, followed by thunder. The lightning strike ripped a gash in the helicopter, hitting Rinne's container next and breaking it open. The helicopter began spinning uncontrollably.

Rinne heard the men shouting.

"No way... We got hit?! Was our route info leaked?!"

"What the hell's going on?!"

"Hold on tight!"

The belts keeping the container in place had snapped when the lightning hit. Centrifugal force generated by the helicopter's spinning pushed the container out of the hatch, which had opened due to a system malfunction.

Rinne saw the night sky through the crack in the damaged container.

"..."

The metal container that held Rinne was plummeting to the ground.

◆

"Loki's tip on the flight path was right."

In a grove in Kokonoe Park in the western part of the city, a girl in a high-collared, long overcoat worn on top of white body armor was talking on her phone, watching the helicopter crash after the lightning strike knocked it off course.

"Wow, that's skill. The pilot must be a genius to control the fall like that. The crew might even survive the crash," the girl commented as nonchalantly as if she was watching a fireworks display.

She was distracted from the helicopter and started doing something on her phone. Around her, several people stood dressed in similar white body armor.

"You landed a clear hit from quite a distance. Neat." The girl praised a man holding a long cannon.

"Thank you, Ritter," he replied.

The man was much older than the girl, but she seemed to be his superior.

"That's a prototype from our lab, no?"

"Yes, it's an artificially engineered factor artillery piece powered by the First Factor's ability and modified for sniping. The factor-charged magazine is the first of its kind, allowing soldiers others than Kampfers to utilize factor powers. Its attack power and precision leave nothing to be desired. The Calamity Research Institute's special armored helicopter was effectively defenseless against—"

"Sorry, I don't care," the girl cut him off, waving dismissively with her free hand.

"Oh, my apologies for rambling on."

"What I want to know is about the dragon girl."

"We've been able to confirm that the container fell out of the helicopter. But whether she survived a fall from that height…"

"You get bears here, apparently."

"Er… Bears?"

The man was confused by the abrupt change of topic.

"An unarmed human is unlikely to win against a bear, no?"

"I…would have to agree…"

"But a mythical girl can kill a bear with her little finger."

"I see, but what does this have to do with…?"

"What I'm saying is, she won't die from a fall from that height. If there was any risk of that, do you think we'd be going ahead with this plan? Fortunately, mythical girls are tough enough to withstand any degree of rough handling."

The girl leaned back in a stretch, her golden hair swaying with her movements.

"Excuse me, Ritter, but...you seem to be lacking focus on our mission..."

"I wish I was flirting with my dearest right now instead of being stuck on this mission."

"With all due respect—"

"Sheesh, I know! Even at my rank, I wouldn't disobey the Order. Did you clear the area of civilians yet?"

"Almost. It's a wide area, but we reckon it's ninety-six percent clear by now. Comms are all set up."

"What's the dragon girl's berserk status?"

"According to Loki, it was stopped at phase one an hour ago through the application of suppressants and cryopreservation."

"'Kay. Instruct Team Two to remain vigilant and secure a safe retreat route."

"Roger. Any orders for the Kampfers?"

"If I end up fighting, the enhanced humans will just get in the way. Have them provide support to Team Two," she commanded, tapping on her smartphone furiously. "Sending messages to my dearest always makes me crave the spotlight. I'll go and capture the dragon miss myself."

She brushed a stray hair away from her cheek.

"What a sad affair, having to capture my doomed kin."

◆

By the time Ryuunosuke finished up the student council work, it was already nighttime. The other student council members had left at the usual time to do their club activities or whatever else they had planned for the day, but Ryuunosuke dutifully stayed behind to complete the tasks Ranko had entrusted to him. He worked himself up into a document-processing frenzy and used that momentum to finish other remaining paperwork as well, leaving the room only when the janitor urged him to go home.

The sky was clear, and the moon was shining brightly. Ryuunosuke went through Kokonoe Park—a large recreation and nature park with walking trails, a pond and a stream, a meadow, playground, and even a designated barbecue area. The boy strode across the grass, his path illuminated by lampposts. On his left-hand side was a small woodland, and on the right-hand side was the pond. He passed a sign warning people about perverts. During the day, the park was full of dog-walkers, but this late at night, there weren't even any joggers. Walking through a deserted park at night might not be the safest thing to do, but for Ryuunosuke, it was a shortcut home.

Kokonoe City was within the Tokyo Metropolitan area, but it wasn't as populous as any of the big cities in the twenty-three special wards. Ryuunosuke's house was in West Kokonoe, built on flat land surrounded by hills. There was very sparsely populated farmland just a short walk from the train station. A town with lots of nature around—that had a nice ring to it. It really didn't feel like Tokyo. A curious thing about Kokonoe was that despite the fact not many people lived there, it had several parks. And there was always some roadwork going on, so the roads were smoother than in most places.

"Huh?"

Ryuunosuke heard a message notification from his phone. He took it out of the pocket of his blazer and saw it was from Mari.

"There's loads…"

She was sending messages one after another and at lighting speed, asking if he was free. Ryuunosuke shuddered.

"*'You've got to go out for ramen with me one of these days! I won't take no for an answer!'* How many stickers did she follow that up with…? How thirsty is she for my attention?"

He wondered for a while about how to reply. Eventually, he settled for a single stamp with a picture of a cartoon poop swirl saying, Good night. No sooner had he closed the messenger app than he heard a notification sound again.

"She's so fast to reply…"

But it wasn't a message from Mari this time. It was an alert from a news site.

"Wait, I don't remember signing up for updates from this site."

He wondered if he'd accidentally tapped something, subscribing without intending to. Upon opening the site, the top headline was about a killer being sentenced to death. Ryuunosuke remembered reading about the murders a few years earlier. Someone kindly lent a man money to help him with his debt, but he ended up killing not only his benefactor but also their family. He even set their house on fire. It was horrible.

The article about the death sentence had a lot of comments from users. Ryuunosuke normally didn't bother reading comments on news sites, but this time, he found himself scrolling through them.

It's the guy who killed that Good Samaritan, isn't it? And they only sentenced him now?
How many more years is he gonna be living off the taxpayers' money?
If I were on the jury, I'd have smashed the kill him button from the start.
Finally closure for the victims' friends and relatives.

Ryuunosuke's eyes lingered on the next comment.

That guy's human garbage, seriously, it began. It was the next line that Ryuunosuke couldn't look away from.

Some people don't deserve to live.

It was just an offhand comment under a news article, reflecting the general consensus about the case. A trite line of no importance. An insensitive thought made public.

And yet these words displayed on the small screen of his phone deeply bothered Ryuunosuke. He thought about that statement, what it meant to him, but he quickly told himself to stop. He knew the answer already.

Ryuunosuke swiped to close the browser and silenced his notifications.

Were some people really so bad that they *had* to be killed?

Ryuunosuke remembered what Mari said to him earlier at the student council meeting.

"You go out of your way to help people even when they don't deserve it."

"Even I wouldn't help a person like that, though," he said to himself. He pictured himself meeting someone everyone thought deserved to die. He imagined that person pleading for help.

"If that happened, I'd…"

It was a lie that helping people was a hobby to Ryuunosuke. He knew full well it went far beyond something that could be classified as a hobby. He had this obsessive sense of duty to help, even if his help wasn't wanted or if it would frustrate or anger the person he insisted on helping. There must have been a reason he was like that, but despite all his soul-searching, he couldn't come up with anything.

A sudden flash of light split the sky, followed by a thunderous rumble that Ryuunosuke felt through his whole body.

"Was that thunder? Is it going to rain? Damn, I didn't bring an umbrella."

The sky was clear. If it wasn't for the fact that it was nighttime, that would've literally been a bolt from the blue. Ryuunosuke scanned the sky but couldn't see any clouds gathering. He did spot something unusual, though: a burning object in the sky, moving erratically.

"Whoa… What the heck am I seeing?"

His eyes lit up with the hope that he was at last witnessing a real UFO. As his eyes adjusted to observe the bright object in the sky, he was late to notice that it was going to crash down near him.

"Wait, huh?!"

It landed just a few meters away.

"Yikes!"

The force of the impact and sheer surprise knocked Ryuunosuke off his feet, and he fell on his butt. The thing that had dropped from the sky kicked up a cloud of dust, so for a moment, he couldn't see anything.

"Ugh! What's going on today...?"

He stood up, coughing. The dust slowly settled, and he could finally see what the thing was—a large container, partially crushed and broken open. Except that Ryuunosuke wasn't looking at it, or at the crater it'd made on the ground where it fell. He was completely transfixed by the person inside it. Moonlight and starlight, along with the artificial sources in the city, illuminated the inside of the container, revealing a person sitting on a chair.

She had long hair and looked so gorgeous, she could be crowned a world-class beauty, but her outfit did not suit her at all—it was a straitjacket. But the fact that this beautiful girl was in a straitjacket wasn't nearly as shocking as the two horns growing from her head, pointing skyward. Ryuunosuke stared at them, and then his gaze slid down to a scaly tail with hard plates jutting from the base of her spine. Underdeveloped wings lacking membranes were growing out of her scapulae. Those weren't body parts any human should possess, which meant the girl wasn't human. The girl brought to mind a certain mythical creature.

"A...dragon?"

The girl looked human to a certain extent, but at the same time, she displayed traits characteristic of dragons from legends. Humans didn't have wings, horns, or tails. They'd either lost them through the process of evolution or hadn't evolved to have them at all. If this girl had them, she was more dragon than human.

The dragon turned toward Ryuunosuke, and their eyes met. It was as if time stopped.

Japan was a modern country, where scientific thinking explained all phenomena, supernatural creatures had been relegated to the realm of imagination, and legends of olden times were understood to be fictional fairy tales.

The boy, Ryuunosuke Dazai.

The girl, Rinne Irako.

Was it a chance meeting, or had fate brought them together?

That night, Ryuunosuke encountered a real mythical girl.

He suddenly heard a voice that didn't belong to anyone he knew.

"Help as many people as you can, for the both of us."

In his mind, he saw rising flames, but that image quickly faded. Strangely, he felt as if he'd heard that voice and seen those flames before. But it was only for a moment.

"You there."

The girl's beautiful voice set time in motion again. Thoughts were speeding through Ryuunosuke's head.

She can't be a dragon, come on. But then what is she? Is she human? Maybe she's a cosplayer. But why would she be cosplaying here, in the middle of the night? Sitting in this metal box? No, it's got to be some sort of incident...or accident?

"Did you not hear me? I am talking to you. There is nobody else here."

She looked at him sharply, and the jumble of thoughts in his mind disappeared at once.

"Huh? You're talking to me? Right, of course. Wh-what do you want from me?"

"I would have expected a humbler attitude... No matter. Come closer and pull this thing out of my back," she commanded imperiously.

It took some time for Ryuunosuke's brain to process what she asked. He was just so shocked that she'd spoken to him.

"What do you mean? Pull what out of your back...?"

He looked at her with a puzzled frown.

"The tube... Urgh..."

"A-are you okay...?"

She panted, unable to continue speaking. Upon closer inspection, beads of perspiration dotted her forehead and she was breathing heavily, appearing exhausted.

"What's going on...?"

Ryuunosuke was still wary, but seeing that the girl was in pain, he couldn't help but walk closer. He approached her as cautiously as if she were a large carnivorous beast bound with chains, stopping within an arm's reach of her.

"Fear not. I am not going to eat you."

She might have meant it as a joke, but somehow, it didn't sound like it to Ryuunosuke. He slowly craned his neck to look at her back.

"Yikes, what's this...?"

Four black conical funnels were sticking out of the straitjacket. One of them had a thick tube attached to it, which was connected to the girl's chair. Three tubes were lying on the ground. They must have been ripped out by the impact when the container crashed.

"You want me to pull this tube out?"

"Yes."

Ryuunosuke crouched behind the girl. He grabbed the tube at the base with one hand, bracing his other against the girl's back. He felt the warmth of her body through the thick fabric of the straitjacket.

Ryuunosuke pulled at the tube forcefully.

"Arrrgh...!"

He stopped immediately when the girl screamed, her face twisted in pain.

"S-sorry! Did I hurt you?"

As hard as it was for him to believe, it seemed the tube was connected to her body.

Ryuunosuke hesitated, unsure of what to do. If this was some special medical device, perhaps he shouldn't be removing it.

"Do not worry, pull it out. Do it in one go."

"Okay."

He made up his mind and pulled at the tube one more time, with all his strength.

"Nnngh... Uh... Nguh!"

The tube felt stuck inside her. Ryuunosuke pulled even harder, and it slowly began to come out.

"Huff... Hngh!"

He managed to pull it out. Like the other tubes, this one had a needle at the end. It was covered in blood. Some blood had splattered on Ryuunosuke's blazer, but he didn't mind.

"A-are you okay?"

"There is no need for concern... You have done well. I appreciate it."

She pushed against her bonds until the metal fastenings of the straitjacket shattered. Once her arms were free, she ripped the rest of the thick belts restraining her as easily as if they were worn-out rubber bands.

Ryuunosuke watched with amazement, but by then, his sense of normalcy had been thrown so out of balance that he simply accepted that this girl was very strong.

The girl leaned back and crossed her legs, eyeing Ryuunosuke haughtily. She made the plain chair look like a throne.

"How many years has it been since my last descent...?"

"..."

The faint glow of streetlights thinned the darkness just enough for Ryuunosuke to see how dangerously beautiful the dragon girl was, and he gasped.

She had long, glossy hair, and a beautiful, adorably doll-like face that somehow also emanated an austere dignity. Her beauty wasn't as instantly dazzling as Mari's, but it was in no way inferior. The dragon girl's beauty was refined, a combination of cherubic softness with fierce elegance and nobility, like ice and fire.

"Well," she said, brushing off the strands of her bangs, which had gotten stuck to her sweaty forehead. "What is your name?"

"Uh... What?"

"I asked for your name. You helped me, and I wish to learn your name before the end."

Ryuunosuke was somewhat perturbed by how ominous that sounded.

"My name is...Ryuunosuke Dazai."

"Ryuunosuke Dazai. A fine name. My name is Rinne. Rinne Irako. You need not remember my name. We will not meet again."

She stood from the chair, then stumbled.

"Careful there!"

Ryuunosuke wasn't usually comfortable being close to girls, but this wasn't an ordinary situation. He reached out with his left hand and caught the girl's wrist.

"Let go!"

"Wha…? Ouch!"

She felt so hot that he reflexively pulled his hand away. Rinne collapsed onto the ground.

"I'm sorry," he said.

Ryuunosuke offered her his hand to help her up, but she ignored him. Her body wasn't hot like from fever—to the boy, it had felt as if he'd touched red-hot iron. His palm was swollen, the skin red as if he'd been burned. A human couldn't be so hot as to burn another.

Rinne's eyes gleamed with prickly hostility, not really directed at Ryuunosuke but the world in general.

"Do not ever touch me without my permission."

She stood up shakily. Then she noticed something.

"What is that…on your hand?"

Ryuunosuke followed her gaze to his left hand. A ring of light had appeared on his ring finger.

"What's this…?" he said, surprised.

Then the ring of light vanished as if it had never been there.

"It cannot be… Why would you have the…?" Rinne began but stopped when she heard a voice nearby.

"This is V. I've located the dragon. She's accompanied by one civilian. I will follow the standard response protocol. Argh, let's get this done and over with, so I can go and get my ramen at Saburou's…"

A girl emerged from the dark grove of trees. She was wearing a black cloak over white body armor. Her long golden pigtails bounced up and down as she walked.

"Wait a second…"

"No way..."

Even in the darkness, Ryuunosuke instantly recognized the pretty blond girl.

"What are you doing here...?"
"Why are you here...?"

Their voices overlapped.

"Abara..."

"Ryuunosuke Dazai..."

Ryuunosuke was the more shocked of the two, his mouth hanging open. He didn't understand why Mari, whom he had seen at the student council meeting a few hours earlier, was in the park at night.

"You *are* Abara, right...?"

It was her, but Ryuunosuke had to ask to make sure, not because reality was getting too weird for his brain to cope with, but because her appearance had changed somewhat. Mari's mouth was slightly open, and he could see two sharp teeth peeking out, like a carnivorous animal's fangs. Mari's ears weren't rounded as usual, but pointy and elongated.

Those were the only differences, but after seeing the dragon girl, Ryuunosuke instantly thought that Mari looked like another mythical creature.

"Are you a...vampire?"

Vampires were nocturnal monsters that were able to transform into bats or wolves. They had no reflection, slept in coffins, hated sunlight and garlic, and used their sharp fangs to attack people and drink blood. Mari, though, seemed perfectly at ease in sunlight, and her favorite food was a hearty bowl of ramen topped with a heap of garlic. She didn't normally have fangs, and Ryuunosuke had, of course, never seen her drinking blood. And yet she looked so much like a vampire.

"First a dragon, now a vampire? It's still a while until Halloween, you know..."

Ryuunosuke couldn't keep up with all the extraordinary events of that day. Rinne also seemed thrown by her unexpected encounter with the boy.

"Ryuunosuke Dazai... Don't tell me you're a member of the Calamity Research Institute...?" Mari asked hesitantly.

"The what now?"

"Right, of course you're not. You just happened to be in the wrong place at the wrong time... So much for clearing civilians from the target area..." Mari tutted. "Now, you'll just do as I say."

"Wh-what do you want?"

"Come over here."

"I'm not moving an inch until you explain what's going on, Abara. Why do you look like this? Is it some sort of cosplay? And if you're going to cosplay, do it in Shibuya, not in a park at night."

"Sorry, but I'm not authorized to explain the situation to civilians. Hurry up and come over to me. If the target resists capture, it's going to end up in a fight. No, it could even escalate to war."

"What on earth are you talking about, Abara—?"

Ryuunosuke stopped abruptly when Rinne stepped in front of him. He couldn't tell if her intention was to interrupt the conversation or protect him.

"You have the gall to chitchat with the boy as if I am not here."

"Hmph!" Mari snorted. "You're not going to obediently surrender, huh?"

"You are a mythical girl with the vampire factor, are you not?"

"...So what if I am?" the vampire replied to the dragon rudely.

"I am Rinne Irako, a mythical girl with the dragon factor."

"I didn't ask."

Mari cocked her head at Rinne's sudden introduction.

"It pains me to have to ask you this, but have you not been taught any manners?" Rinne asked in response to Mari's bluntness.

"What are you getting at? Trying to rile me up, huh?"

"I would have thought it a common courtesy to introduce oneself to the opponent before a duel."

"What are you, a medieval general?"

"Ah, my mistake. I should have gathered from your daft appearance that you are a simpleton. I must apologize for overestimating your IQ."

"I-I'm going to freaking tear you to pieces!" Mari shouted, a blue vein popping out on her temple.

Meanwhile, Rinne remained calm. Or at least, she was expressionless.

"I was not trying to...provoke you...," Rinne replied.

Her breathing was shallow, laborious. Beads of sweat rolled down her face. Even just standing upright seemed like a lot of effort for her.

"Fine, whatever. I'll tell you my name so that you'll know who defeated you. I'm Mari Vlad Abara, a vampire mythical girl."

"Mari Vlad Abara. A name I shall remember."

"Rinne Irako... You annoy the hell out of me, but I'll remember your name, too."

The atmosphere became so thick with tension, you could cut it with a knife. Sensing that each side was waiting for the other to make the slightest move, Ryuunosuke hurriedly stepped in to stop the impending violence.

"H-hey, girls. You're not really going to fight, right?"

"You stay out of this. Step away," Rinne said, grabbing him by his belt. "Whether it is my destiny to lose or win, I do not know, but I will not surrender without a fight. Besides...an encounter between mythical girls with conflicting interests does not lead to a simple struggle."

Rinne roughly pulled on his belt.

"It leads to war."

"Aaah!"

That quick tug was enough to send Ryuunosuke flying. He curled up defensively and rolled when he hit the ground. The girl was about his age, and smaller than him, but she had flung him as if he were a stuffed toy. To think she was able to do that in her condition, struggling to stay upright. Ryuunosuke couldn't believe it.

"You'd better listen to the half-dead dragon, Ryuunosuke Dazai. This isn't a place for humans right now. Be good and go take a seat somewhere."

"But why do you have to fight?! What's the reason? Tell me, because I don't see any!"

"A reason…?"

"Why do we have to…?"

They both reacted as if he was the one not making any sense.

"The only reason we need is that we're both here," Rinne said.

Mari raised her arm to the sky.

"Let's change into something more comfortable! Immortal Queen!"

On that cue, Mari's clothes began to transform. They unraveled, turning into bloodred threads that wove together into a crimson formal dress, opera gloves a tone darker, and scarlet pumps with high heels. A red tiara appeared on Mari's head, eye-catching against her blond hair. The skirt of her dress fluttered in a gust of wind. She looked beautiful and majestic, elegant yet menacing, refined yet showy.

"Is this your Valkyrie Dress…?" Rinne asked.

"That's right! My special Valkyrie Dress, Immortal Queen. Why don't you put on yours? A girl's got to look her best on the battlefield. I'll wait."

Rinne shook her head.

"I am ready."

"If you say so. I guess nobody would be so stupid as to let you make off with a Valkyrie Dress or any weapons. You've been tranquilized, too. You're not going to complain it's not fair that I'm attacking you in your sorry state?"

"It is not unfair to use one's advantages in battle."

"Good, we agree on something. Just so you know, if you surrender and promise to be good, I won't hurt you too much."

"You must be delirious to think such an offer would tempt me."

"Fine, I'll pound you into pulp. It's been something of a dream for me to just go at it with a dragon."

Rinne pointed at Mari's face.

"You have a high nose bridge."

"Huh? So what? My nose is cute."

"I shall remodel your face to make it even cuter."

That triggered Mari.

"I'll...!" She dragged the long nails of her left hand on the palm of her right, splitting the skin open. "...friggin'...!" Then she raised her right hand, opening her fingers. "...kill you!

"Carmilla, the Bloody Maiden!"

Blood gushed from the cut on Mari's hand, solidifying into the shape of a strange weapon that looked like the combination of a spear, an ax, and a scythe. The red polearm was some kind of a halberd or a war scythe, or perhaps the best way to describe it would be as a halberd scythe.

Mari was holding the long weapon in one hand. She swung it with ease, and the huge blade swooshed through the air, leaving behind a bloody trail.

Seeing his schoolmate do an outfit transformation and summon a giant weapon took a toll on Ryuunosuke's sanity.

"This can't be real... Why is today getting weirder and weirder...?" he muttered to himself.

Mari leaped up, bat wings appearing on her back. She was heading straight for the wounded dragon, accelerating with a great flap of her wings. She raised her Bloody Maiden dramatically, aiming the giant ax edge toward the ground.

"I'm supposed to capture you alive, so I'll do my best to be gentle... Sorry in advance if my hand slips."

The vampire girl began to spin her weapon around, looking like a red tornado to Ryuunosuke. She was handling that unwieldy weapon as if it were a little twig. Its triple blades were approaching Rinne at high speed.

"I...didn't think anyone could move so fast that eyes couldn't follow..."

All Ryuunosuke could see was a red blur. He was standing near Rinne and could feel the gusts of wind stirred by Mari's rapid, dance-like movements with the weapon.

"A scythe Reginleif... She created both the dress and the weapon herself...using the vampire factor's blood-manipulation ability...?"

Rinne was analyzing the situation, standing right in the middle of the red tornado.

"Good guess, but you're off the mark. You can't make a sturdy weapon like this just with blood manipulation. My Reginleif, Nosferatu, is augmented through vampire factor blood manipulation and blood creation together. The Bloody Maiden is just one of the forms it can take. That's why I can do things like this, too."

In an instant, her weapon melted into liquid.

"The Impaler!"

The liquefied weapon took on a new form, solidifying into bloody spikes, which Mari sent flying at Rinne. The dragon girl shattered them with kicks and tail swings.

Mari had leaped up into the air while launching her Impaler. Blood that had drenched the ground flew back toward her hand, turning into the Bloody Maiden once more. She attacked Rinne, who continuously dodged the spear thrusts, ax swings, and scythe sweeps but suffered increasing injuries. Specks of her blood sprayed around.

"Hmph! Nice evasion, but you can't keep it up forever!" Mari teased.

Rinne was, in fact, already at her limit.

Mari began to spin her polearm vertically like a twirling baton. Rinne's short reach put her at a disadvantage, so she tried to lunge at Mari, but the vampire girl had been waiting precisely for that. She thrust the Bloody Maiden at Rinne's solar plexus.

"Argh…!"

The strike sent Rinne flying like a soccer ball. She fell on her back next to the metal container, the impact knocking all the air from her lungs. But she sprang to her feet and grabbed the vessel.

"I'll get you now!" she shouted, lifting the container, which must have weighed hundreds of kilograms—no, maybe even several tonnes.

She threw the container, along with the dirt stuck to it, at Mari.

"Somebody pinch me!" Ryuunosuke shouted, shocked by what he'd just witnessed.

The heavy metal box flew straight at Mari, but it didn't hit her. There was an earsplitting sound.

"You're really running out of ideas, huh?" she said mockingly, having sliced the container in half with the Bloody Maiden. Specks of blood still hovered in the air, marking the arc of the weapon's sweep.

Mari began sauntering toward Rinne, the moon shining behind her back. There was a loud *thud* as the two halves of the container landed on the ground.

"…"

Rinne fell to her knees. She had to brace her hands against the ground for support.

"Looks like you're in a lot of pain. Makes me wonder what use you'll be to anyone if you're already half dead."

Mari stopped in front of Rinne and looked down at her.

"You're at berserk phase one, your dragon heart's overheating, and the tranquilizer's side effects have kicked in. You really are unwell, aren't you? I'm impressed you put up a fight at all… On second thought, you shouldn't even have been able to stand up," the vampire said with pity.

Rinne was panting heavily.

"But I can't hold back just because you're not at your best today. That's the code I go by. You might think it's dishonorable, but I just think the stronger side should win."

Rinne's face was drenched with sweat. Even breathing seemed agonizing. And no wonder—Ryuunosuke had felt how insanely hot her body was when he touched her earlier. She was in no condition to fight to begin with, and now she'd also suffered additional injuries all over her body.

"The dragon factor's regenerative ability is supposed to be better than the vampire's, but it looks like suppressing your berserk phase also stops it from working correctly. I'd have recovered from that almost instantly."

The vampire swung around her bloodred weapon. It cut the air with a high-pitched *swish*.

"Don't get me wrong, I do feel sorry for you. I'm just doing my job, though. It's nothing personal."

The giant scythe blade sliced through flesh. Blood spattered into the darkness of the night.

"No…"

Mari gasped in disbelief. It wasn't Rinne she had struck.
"Ryuunosuke…Dazai…"
Ryuunosuke had jumped in to shield Rinne. The scythe cut deeply into his arm.
"Ngh…!"
His eyes widened. He jerked his arm away. Blood trailed down to his hand, dripping from his fingers onto the ground.
"No… Why… Why did you…?"
Ryuunosuke was sweating profusely. He forced himself to smile.
"You haven't killed me, Abara. Don't look so horrified. It's just a little scratch; I'll be fine. I'm your senior—you've got nothing on me."
He was putting on a brave face, knowing full well that she had sliced through major veins and nerves in his arm.
"Abara, I guess I don't really know who you are, but you're also my junior, and I can't condone this behavior."
His injury was serious, but it didn't hurt as much as he'd expected. A spike of adrenaline had numbed the pain.
"I'm going to protect this girl. Leave her alone, Abara. If not…"
Ryuunosuke raised his uninjured arm and took a fighting stance.
"…I'm going to personally fight you off!"
His voice was shaking. Hopeless as it might be, he was desperate to shield Rinne. As for her, she was watching him from behind, narrowing her eyes as if he were a ray of bright light piercing the gloom and doom of her situation. The world had decided everyone would be better off with her dead, but this one boy was trying to save her.
"Thank you," she said quietly, but the wind blew away her words before they could reach him.
The dragon girl's eyes lit up with determination. The glimmer of hope was faint, but it was there. She stood and leaped upward. A cloud

of dust and sand rose around Mari like a small cyclone, solidifying into a wall.

"What...?!"

Mari was unable to see what was going on around her. She was still reeling from the shock of having hurt her crush, so she wasn't thinking clearly. She froze, expecting an attack, but that wasn't why Rinne had walled her off—she'd done that to escape.

"Wh-whoa?!" Ryuunosuke exclaimed.

"We must get away quickly..."

Rinne had lifted Ryuunosuke up onto her shoulders and was running off with him into the thicket.

"Argh! Vampire Knights of Sigismund! Capture them!" Mari shouted in outrage.

Ryuunosuke saw blood rise from the ground and transform into knights in armor. They gave chase, their armor clattering, but they weren't as fast as the dragon girl. The landscape was a blur to Ryuunosuke, who kept bobbing up and down, carried by Rinne. Every now and again, he'd bump into one of her hard horns.

"Why are we running away? I'm sure we could come to an agreement with Abara if we only talked things through—"

"Be quiet, unless you want to bite your tongue and die. You have no right to... No, I did not mean to say that..."

Rinne shook her head.

"Talking to that girl is pointless. Even if you convinced her to side with you, it would not make a difference at this juncture. Since you got involved, she would not be able to just let you go. The Order would not tolerate it. I will not allow them to capture you. We are not running away like cowards—we are buying time."

"Who are those Order people...?"

They ran through the woodland and out onto a plaza, where Rinne finally stopped behind a large ginkgo tree growing at the center. She gently set Ryuunosuke on the ground. She was struggling for air, as if she was dying. She didn't seem just in pain, but actually on the verge of death. It was obvious at a glance that she was on her last legs. It wasn't because of the wounds she'd suffered. There were many, but none were critical. Something else was killing her.

Rinne was sweating nonstop, but her body wasn't cooling down. Her face was bright red, as if someone had dumped hot water on her. Even though she was mostly expressionless, her suffering showed through. Ryuunosuke could feel the heat radiating from her body without touching her. And, on top of that, she had those wounds all over.

But let's not forget that Ryuunosuke, too, was wounded.

"Oww…!"

Once the fear and agitation from earlier died down, the sharp pain that his adrenaline had been suppressing hit him with a vengeance.

Rinne looked at his right arm.

"You are bleeding out…"

The blood wouldn't stop flowing, and with it, Ryuunosuke's life was draining away.

"I wish to ask you a question."

"Y-yeah, sure?"

Ryuunosuke was in so much pain, it took all his self-restraint not to scream. He didn't want the girl to think he was pitiful.

"Tell me why you protected me. You could have stayed out of it and not gotten hurt. You have no reason to be my ally."

"You want to know the reason, huh?"

That voice he couldn't match to any person he knew replayed in his mind.

"Help as many people as you can, for the both of us."

"…I protected you because I wanted to. I don't need a reason to help others."

He made it sound so casual.

Rinne gasped at his reply, deeply moved. Of course, Ryuunosuke had no idea how much what he'd said mattered to her, and he didn't think much of it, either.

It was a lie that helping people was a hobby to him. He was driven by a strong sense of duty to help. For as long as he had that voice stuck in his head, he'd keep helping others at whatever cost to himself. It was a cruel destiny. A self-destructive path. Yet he'd stay on it, for as long as there were people he could assist.

"...Ah, so you are a hopeless altruist."

"People say that to me all the time."

Rinne's breathing became more even. She looked at Ryuunosuke. Beams of moonlight made their way down between the leaves and branches of the ginkgo tree and illuminated the two of them. Rinne could clearly see her reflection in the boy's eyes. Her face in the reflection was no longer displaying hostility.

"I believe you," she said. She closed her eyes briefly, and when she opened them again, she looked Ryuunosuke directly in the eyes. "You are no longer just an unfortunate bystander. If the Order captures you, there is no telling what they might do. And I do not have much time left. Ryuunosuke, listen carefully to what I have to say."

"O-okay, go on…"

"You see…," she began uncomfortably. "This is something I can only ask of you and no one else. The light I saw around your finger when we met convinced me of it."

"Ask away. I'll do whatever I can."

"You do mean it?"

"I never go back on what I say."

"Very well."

Under the night sky, she said to him:

"Wed me."

Sweat drops were running down Rinne's face, but her eyes were intense, determined.

"Sorry, I think I misheard…?"

Ryuunosuke was lightheaded from blood loss, and a marriage proposal was the last thing he'd expected in those circumstances, so he couldn't make sense of what she'd said. He'd probably doubt his hearing even if she'd said it on a perfectly normal day, though.

"I am at my limit. You will soon bleed out to death. This is the only way," she insisted. "Wed me."

It sounded like a bizarre joke. Except that Rinne's voice was dead serious.

"You have the right to refuse, Ryuunosuke. It is a pact that will most likely bring new difficulties into your life. Once you make the decision—even though you don't know what it fully entails—you will not be able to undo it. But right now, you can decide whether to take my offer or leave it. I cannot tell you what hardships to expect after taking the vows. Yet I will make you this offer: Face the adversities the future brings with me, and I swear upon my life to protect you. Perhaps that was too vague. Save the world, Ryuunosuke. By saving me."

No other proposal could have been as effective on Ryuunosuke.

"It sounds crazy, to be honest…"

He gazed back into her golden eyes.

"Are you sure I can save you by doing this?"

Rinne nodded solemnly.

"Okay, then."

Ryuunosuke nodded without further hesitation.

Rinne considered him for a moment before saying, "Thank you." Then she suddenly ripped open the front of the straitjacket, exposing her bare skin to the air.

"Wait… What are you doing…?!"

A glowing red symbol appeared on her delicate chest, centered on her breastbone. Soon after Ryuunosuke saw it, he felt something on his left ring finger. He looked down at it—a pale ring of light had formed around the base of his finger, just like before. The pattern on the ring resembled the symbol on Rinne's chest.

"What is this…?"

"It is what they call the Sacred Sealing Ring, if I am not mistaken."

"The…Sacred Sealing Ring?"

"I have been told that such a ring of light appearing around the ring finger possesses the power to suppress evil, at the cost of sharing the burden of sin we mythical girls carry. If my assumption is correct, you must touch your Sacred Sealing Ring to the Stigma on my chest and make your vow for our marriage to become official. I do not know why you possess the ring…but this is our only hope."

"T-touch your chest?!"

While Ryuunosuke was willing to agree to everything else, he objected to that part. It wasn't only because he got burned from touching her last time. For some reason, touching the glowing symbol on her chest seemed sacrilegious, unforgivable.

"I grant you my permission," she said in a benevolent tone. "You may touch me."

They heard clattering from the direction of the dark woodland— Mari's Vampire Knights had almost caught up to them. Ryuunosuke had to make his decision quickly. She was waiting, gazing at him with urgency in her eyes, which silenced his internal objections—that he feared burning his hand, that he didn't feel comfortable with the idea of touching her chest, or that it was all just too weird.

"Okay, I'm going to touch you…"

"Please proceed."

He reached toward her chest. The closer his fingers were to her skin, the more intense the heat radiated from her. The light around his ring finger also intensified, enveloping his hand in an intricate pattern that made him think of an electric circuit.

He touched her.

Images flashed in his mind—the darkness of the night, flames, a girl, a burning house. There was a sensation of powerlessness, and someone's voice. It lasted only for a moment.

Rinne closed her eyes and began speaking as if in prayer.

"In sickness and in health, in joy and in sorrow, for richer and for poorer…"

He recognized what she was saying as wedding vows.

"…do you vow to stand by my side, to be my support, my companion, and my ally until death do us part?"

With each word, the light around Ryuunosuke's ring finger became hotter. It rose like a flame, burning his finger.

"Say *I do!*" she prompted him.

"I... I do!"

Their fate was sealed.

A ring of light appeared around Rinne's ring finger. A glowing tiara in the same color materialized on her head briefly—and then its light dispersed, disappearing.

Other effects soon followed. The wounds on Rinne's body were healing, and her infernally high temperature was dropping. Ryuunosuke was also affected.

"Huh? My arm... How's this possible?"

His injury was healing rapidly, as if in response to Rinne's own recovery.

"Since we are now wed, you share my regenerative ability."

Rinne closed and opened her fists tentatively.

"Thanks to you...," she began.

She was no longer a pitiful wounded dragon. She was radiating power.

"...I am now this planet's apex predator."

◆

Mari spread her wings, which she'd created from blood, and ran in pursuit of the dragon and the boy. The wings boosted her speed. Vampires could fly in short bursts, but their blood wings weren't really meant for that.

"I can't transform my body to have real wings like dragons and phoenixes, so I'll have to make do with this..."

Mari admitted she'd made a mistake letting the dragon girl escape after she used that dirt-wall trick. She hadn't been thinking logically and went on the defensive for no reason. It was a mistake she could correct, though. Her Vampire Knights of Sigismund were excellent trackers. All

she needed to do was follow them. The dragon girl was too weak to have run far, and in her frail state, she might even lose to the Vampire Knights. The scent of the dragon's blood in the air would lead Mari to her prey for sure.

"The botched berserk suppressant stops her factor from manifesting fully. As long as she can't use her wings to fly away, I can catch up to her. It's just a matter of time. And she knows this, or at least, I'd hope so…"

What preoccupied her more than the chase was the matter of Ryuunosuke, though. Her mission had to take priority, but…

"I'm so sorry, Ryuunosuke Dazai…"

Getting her beloved Ryuunosuke involved in the fight and injuring him wasn't something she could justify to herself. Mission or not, what she'd done was unforgivable. She'd withdrawn her blade as soon as she realized she'd struck Ryuunosuke, so she didn't end up lopping off his arm, but the injury was serious. He might die from it.

Mari knew she'd messed up. It wasn't the first time she'd inadvertently gotten him dragged into something that wasn't his business.

"Ryuunosuke Dazai…"

Even if he recovered from that wound, the Order would be after him, since he'd interfered with the mission. Mari couldn't do anything to prevent that. She supposed the best-case scenario would be Ryuunosuke having his memories erased. As long as he wasn't killed, even if she never saw him again, she'd be okay with that.

"A stupidly altruistic Goody Two-shoes getting involved in my mission was the last thing I needed…"

Suddenly, there was a flash of light through the trees. Mari sensed that all her knights had been annihilated.

"What?! How come?!"

She finally made it to the edge of the woods and emerged into an open area with a large ginkgo tree in the middle.

"…"

There she stopped to observe and get a handle on the situation. She spotted Ryuunosuke and Rinne by the big tree. Rinne looked different. Gone were the wounds and blood that had covered her before, and she showed no sign of deadly exhaustion or weakness. Her wings had membranes. She was fully capable of flight.

"She's healed... Did she recover her dragon factor abilities? Hold on, what's that...?"

Something else attracted Mari's attention—there was no red symbol on Rinne's chest, but there was a red ring of light on her left ring finger. Ryuunosuke, too, had a ring of light on his ring finger. Mari knew exactly what it was.

"Those rings of light... You've got to be kidding me. Sacred Sealing Rings?!"

She stared at the shining rings as if they were a miracle.

"I can't believe it... They're real...," she said to herself.

The dragon took a step toward her.

"You are strong," she said in a voice that now sounded majestic.

The change in her was dramatic—the emaciated, frail dragon had recovered her dignity, power, and confidence.

"I loathe to admit this, but you are strong."

Mari looked at Ryuunosuke, who was standing behind Rinne. His arm looked perfectly fine. His wound, which would have absolutely needed surgery, had simply disappeared. Mari guessed that the Sacred Sealing Ring allowed Rinne to share her regenerative powers with Ryuunosuke.

"..."

She waited in silence for the dragon girl to get to the point.

"You are strong...but I have Ryuunosuke," said Rinne. "I win."

"Oh, really?"

For the first time since her encounter with the dragon, Mari readied herself for battle with deadly seriousness. Her air of nonchalance and playfulness vanished. She bent her knees, crouching slightly, with Carmilla the Bloody Maiden pointed at the ground.

Rinne extended one arm forward.

"You shall witness the power of linked souls."

She clasped her wrist with her other hand.

"Feed on malice...," she called forth her Valkyrie Dress.

*   *   *

"...Nidhoggr!"

The remains of Rinne's straitjacket burst into blue and black flames that enveloped her entire body. They transformed into armor, which looked as if it was made from dragon scales and scutes. It was minimalist, covering only the most vital areas—a scale breastplate with tassets attached, elbow-length gauntlets, greaves that seemed to be made from bony plates and had long talons. The armor was designed not to restrict her wings and tail.

"Huh, so you have your Valkyrie Dress. What a bright idea, equipping a death row convict with that... Well, whatever. Look at you—your outfit's kind of skimpy, don't you think?"

In contrast to Mari's gorgeous crimson dress, Rinne's armor exposed more than it covered. Its defensive qualities seemed rather dubious.

"Why should I wear brittle armor when I have my tough scales? I am satisfied with my dress."

"Oh, really?"

Thus began the second round of their battle. Rinne whipped her tail against the ground and spread her wings. She and Mari leaped simultaneously. They flew at each other in a straight line, at top speed. Mari brandished her polearm, which gave her a range advantage over the unarmed Rinne. But if the vampire had her special weapon, it would only be reasonable to expect the dragon to have something, too.

"Gram!" Rinne shouted, and her right gauntlet transformed.

A new part had been added to her armor—when Rinne extended her arm to the side, a light blade appeared from the back of her hand, its glow dazzlingly bright in the darkness of the night. Besides serving to protect Rinne's hand, the gauntlet was also the hilt of her sword.

Mari took a swing at Rinne with the ax blade of her polearm. Rinne blocked it with her sword.

"Is that your little 'claw,' dragon?!"

Rinne didn't reply.

"Hnnngh!"

She flung Mari away.

"She's monstrously strong...!" Mari admitted and tutted angrily as she flew backward.

Among all the mythical factors, the vampire factor was one of the most powerful when it came to physical abilities. Mari had absolute confidence in her strength. Her brief exchange of blows with the dragon in her restored form taught her a valuable lesson—that dragons were in a league of their own. Like a passenger car and a dump truck.

Rinne changed her stance. She put one foot forward and crouched, leaned slightly toward her opponent, and covered her right arm with her left as if she were a samurai ready to draw their sword.

"...!"

A chill ran down Mari's spine. She held the Bloody Maiden in front of her defensively. If it weren't for her superhuman senses and battle experience, she'd have had her head chopped off just then.

A slash of the dragon's sword smudged the darkness with a light blur. She was about ten meters away from Mari. Her sword's reach was maybe one meter, so Mari should've been safe at that distance. Yet somehow, the strike felled the great ginkgo tree and reached Mari's neck. The Bloody Maiden, which Mari used to protect herself, snapped loudly in half and, losing its rigidity, turned into blood, which splashed onto the ground, creating a large puddle.

Mari landed on the ground.

"Looks like I've got to stop fooling around and fight you for real," she said, raising her arm. "Vampire Knights of Sigismund!"

The puddle of blood around her roiled. Blood knights began to rise from it, armored and armed with swords or spears, carrying shields. A great number of them rushed Rinne all at once.

"Your ridiculous strength won't be much use to you if you can't get close to me!"

Unlike Mari's first batch of Vampire Knights, which had been optimized for speed and pursuit, these were bigger and more numerous. Rinne, though, didn't even try to dodge the oncoming throng. She had her eyes fixed on Mari. She silently extended her right arm, and her sword of light disappeared. The opening on her gauntlet the sword had retreated into was glowing.

"You underestimate dragons, assuming they can only fight at close range."

The gauntlet, which had also turned out to be a sword hilt, had another use—it was a turret.

"Fafnir!" the dragon girl roared.

A beam of blue light shot out of the gauntlet, growing hotter and expanding to engulf the Vampire Knights as it flew straight at Mari.

"Shit…!" Mari swore, but her curse was drowned out by the blast as the beam hit.

Ryuunosuke had silently watched the girls' battle from beginning to end. It was now over. When the dust cloud cleared, he saw Mari lying on the ground. She was alive but had taken heavy damage. Her red dress had vanished, and she was back in her body armor and cloak.

Mari sat up, but when she tried to stand, she staggered and dropped to her knees. She stared at Rinne's gauntlet with vacant eyes.

"You redirected the surplus heat from your dragon heart into that dragon breath Reginleif."

"If I spare you, you will come after me again someday. In which case, I have no choice…"

The beam of light shone out of Rinne's gauntlet again. She walked toward Mari, stopping right in front of her. She raised her arm and brought it down swiftly.

Mari had suffered too much damage to be able to dodge or block the strike. She needed more time to recover her mobility. She shut her eyes.

"No, wait!"

It was like déjà vu. Ryuunosuke jumped out in front of Rinne to shield Mari.

The blade of light stopped just a centimeter away from Ryuunosuke.

"You asked me for help, and I agreed, but I didn't want to lend you a hand to finish off Abara. I simply wanted to save you and myself. Don't hurt Abara anymore, or I'll do all I can to protect her from you. I know what you're thinking: I keep flip-flopping…"

Ryuunosuke was determined to protect Mari this time, even if it meant dying to Rinne's blade.

"Think what you want, but I can't stand by and watch my friend get killed."

"Ryuunosuke…Dazai…," Mari whispered behind him.

Ryuunosuke had no idea she was looking at him with eyes sparkling with love.

"But leaving her alive is too risky…," Rinne began but didn't finish, sensing that Ryuunosuke was in a lifesaving frenzy and wouldn't back down. "Very well, we shall spare her. I will restrain and deliver her to the Calamity Research Institute."

Rinne withdrew her blade into the gauntlet.

"As if I'd let you, fool!" Mari shouted as soon as the dragon's weapon disappeared.

She jumped up high into the sky, spread her wings, and flew away.

"Sto—" Rinne didn't finish.

She tried to chase the vampire girl, but suddenly, all strength had left her. Her armor, wings, horns, and tail dissolved into thin air. She was again dressed in the tattered straitjacket.

Rinne's legs buckled under her, and she fell to her knees, looking like a vulnerable young girl.

"Hey, are you okay?!"

Ryuunosuke managed to catch her before she collapsed on the ground. Her body was no longer abnormally hot. She was breathing evenly, asleep.

"She ran out of battery and conked out… That's a happy ending…I guess?"

The battle had ended, but it wasn't over yet. A whole pile of new problems had been left behind.

"Abara…"

Ryuunosuke gazed in the direction Mari had flown. His meeting with Mari that night was a shock, and the extraordinary chain of events had tired him out. No wonder he wasn't alert enough to notice the sound of engines.

Several black vans stopped in front of him, blinding him with the headlights.

"The hell... What now...?!"

Ryuunosuke instinctively shielded his eyes from the glare. The van doors opened abruptly, and a squad of armored people with automatic guns poured out of them to surround Ryuunosuke and Rinne. To the boy, they looked like special police forces. One of them aimed at Ryuunosuke.

"Stay where you are! Kneel on the ground with your hands up!"

That wasn't the kind of thing Ryuunosuke would've expected to hear from police officers. These armed people had to be some other group.

"..."

Ryuunosuke had no choice but to do as he'd been told. When he'd knelt, two people got out of the van directly opposite him. He couldn't see them well because of the headlights, but they clearly looked different from the others. One was a young girl in a white lab coat.

"Well, well, look at this mess. I made the right call supplying her with the Valkyrie Dress just in case," she said in a sleepy voice.

"You armed the Third Factor? Isn't a decision like that outside your authority, *Deputy* Chief Researcher...?" the other person, a tall man wearing a suit, replied to her.

"Sarashina, it was better to have her equipped than not. The fact that she fought off the Order agents is proof of that, no? I still don't understand how they found out about the transport route, though..."

The girl cocked her head quizzically.

"Well, the transporter is totaled, but there were zero casualties, and Rinne is alive and well, so nobody has a reason to complain, no? Rinne would've been unable to use her Valkyrie Dress in her uncontrolled state anyway, and if I hadn't equipped her, it would've ended up being an even bigger mess. The end result proves my course of action was correct."

"I'm not entirely convinced... Is it just me, or has the Third Factor's berserk phase gone down?"

"Yup. We'll need to examine her later, but at a glance, I can tell you that it looks as if it has been completely nullified."

The girl in the lab coat walked over to Ryuunosuke... No, it was Rinne she was walking toward. Without the strong light behind her, Ryuunosuke could finally see her face. Foolish of him to have thought that day couldn't bring any more surprises.

"P-President...?"

"Shush."

Ranko Akeda, the student council president, silenced him, putting her index finger on his lips. He saw that she still wore her school uniform under the unbuttoned lab coat. The coat was too big for her, the sleeves longer than her arms.

Ranko took out a penlight from the breast pocket of her lab coat. She lifted Rinne's eyelids and shone the light in each eye. Next, she checked Rinne's pulse. *Like a doctor*, it occurred to Ryuunosuke.

"It looks like she used up her factor energy, wearing herself out... Her mythical factor is now dormant. I also see that her Stigma has disappeared. Blood pressure, pulse, and temperature are all normal. Her DF value is also within norm... It's almost as if..."

Ranko took Rinne's left hand in hers to examine a dark mark around her ring finger. The ring of light, which shone so brightly in battle, had vanished when Rinne fell asleep.

"No friggin' way!" Ranko suddenly exclaimed.

She quickly covered her mouth with her hands, looking around anxiously.

"S-sorry, never mind what I just said."

"Er... President?" Ryuunosuke asked, raising his hand timidly. "Can you tell me why you're here?"

"Sorry, this must be a shock for you, but don't worry—we're not going to hurt you. We're from the Special Calamity Prevention Research Institute, also known as Calamity Research Institute for short."

Calamity Research Institute—Ryuunosuke had heard the name earlier that night. Both Rinne and Mari had mentioned it. Ryuunosuke guessed that Rinne also belonged to that organization.

Ranko looked at Ryuunosuke's left hand. He also had a dark mark around his ring finger, like a bruise or birthmark.

"I see what happened here. Sorry, Dazai boy, but I'll have you come with me to answer some questions."

"Wait, I'm not going any—," he began, but Ranko directed her penlight at his eyes and, with one pink flash, sent him into a deep slumber.

"Thank you…"

Before his consciousness completely faded, Ryuunosuke caught Ranko's tearful words of gratitude.

CHAPTER 2

Apoptosis of Humanity's Happiness

"Huh?!"

Ryuunosuke woke up on a bed in a room illuminated by LED lights on a high ceiling. He looked around to see where he was, but there were white hospital curtains all around him.

"What is this place...?"

He wondered if it was, in fact, a hospital. It could well be one, based on what little he could see and the medicinal smell in the air. He felt woozy, maybe because he'd only just woken.

"...Huh?"

Something was not right. Ryuunosuke found he couldn't sit up. Worse, he couldn't even roll to the side. He managed to lift his head at least and saw he was tied to the bed with belts, and he'd been changed out of his school uniform into a hospital gown. The uniform was neatly folded on top of a medical trolley next to the bed.

"What happened to me...?"

Slowly, the haze in his head cleared, and he remembered the dragon girl and the vampire girl, the battle in the park, and the armed group that turned up after with Ranko, who had flashed a strange light into his eyes...

"You've woken up?" came a male voice.

The curtains opened, and Ryuunosuke recognized the man in a suit from that night, except he was no longer wearing a suit, but a white shirt with a lab coat over it. The man was holding a device that looked like an LCD tablet.

"My name is Suberu Sarashina. I am a medical researcher. May I ask how you're feeling? Any headache or nausea?"

"Um, no, I'm fine... My head feels a bit heavy, but that's it."

"That's a hypnosis side effect. Nothing to worry about—it will pass shortly."

"Oh, I also injured my arm...," Ryuunosuke began, but he stopped when he craned his neck to look at his arm.

Mari's attack had left a large scar, but the wound had healed. He could move his hand without any pain.

Ah, right. It healed on its own in that flash of light after the marriage vows...

Suberu called someone on the intercom next to the bed.

"Sarashina here. The boy is awake. Yes. Yes, of course."

He hung up and began to unbuckle the belts restraining Ryuunosuke.

"My apologies for strapping you to the bed. Regulations, you understand."

Finally free, Ryuunosuke sat on the edge of the bed.

"So...what is this place?"

It wasn't the man who replied to him, though.

"Allow me to explain."

The student council president, Ranko, had entered the room, still dressed in her school uniform with a lab coat over it. She had an ID on a lanyard this time.

"Sarashina, please take this report to the higher-ups."

"Sure."

The man left the room.

"President..."

"Don't call me that. Here, I'm the deputy chief... Well, I guess it doesn't matter. Call me anything you want."

"So it wasn't a dream after all... You're here, too."

"You hadn't dreamed it, Dazai boy."

She acted exactly the same as she did at school. The only thing different about her was that oversize lab coat.

"I must inform you of something important first."

"Yeah?"

"You're no longer a denizen of an ordinary world. Returning to everyday life as you'd known it is impossible."

"Right..."

He remembered what Rinne had said to him earlier.

"It is a pact that will most likely bring new difficulties into your life."

At the time, he hadn't really considered whether he was ready for such big changes in his life. He just wanted to put a stop to the dramatic events of that night—to save the girl. He didn't regret his choice, because it achieved what he'd wanted at that moment.

"Yeah, I knew it was a path of no return." Ryuunosuke tried to sound nonchalant about it.

"Good." Ranko nodded, satisfied. "We are in the third district of West Kokonoe, Kokonoe City, Tokyo Metropolis. Do you know the Kokonoe Biochemical Research Institute?"

"West Kokonoe, third district...?"

That wasn't far from West Kokonoe Park, where Rinne and Mari had fought. District Three was mostly hills.

"Wait, is it on top of the big hill?"

Ryuunosuke remembered exploring that area together with his friend Aya when they were in elementary school. The No Entry signboards and surveillance cameras dotted around the place had been particularly memorable.

"Correct. And it's exactly the sort of facility you've probably imagined. Built on the big hill, much of it goes deep underground. We're inside that hill. The subterranean part of the complex is called the Underground Kokonoe Factor Research Facility. This is the sick bay. You've been asleep for two hours."

"The Underground Kokonoe Factor Research Facility, huh…"

Ryuunosuke gazed up at the ceiling.

The sick bay had no windows. It might well be underground, or it might not be.

"I'm the deputy chief medical researcher here at the Underground Kokonoe Factor Research Facility of the Special Calamity Prevention Research Institute."

"Deputy chief medical researcher…?"

"My schoolgirl alter ego is just a cover. Sorry for deceiving you."

Ranko smiled awkwardly and scratched her cheek.

Ryuunosuke had no idea how important her position was, but based on how Suberu treated her with deference, she had a higher status here and might even be an adult.

"I can't help thinking that you're just the student council president I know you as, and this is some elaborate joke…"

"It'll take you some time to adjust, I suppose."

Ryuunosuke looked her up and down. She didn't give off the impression she was some deputy chief medical researcher. In all honesty, she didn't even look like a high schooler. She was so small and seemed so young, anyone would assume she was in elementary school.

"Sorry… I can't picture you as a researcher…"

"Well, all girls have their secrets. Appearances can be deceiving."

Ranko poked his cheek with her index finger.

"I'm moonlighting as a high schooler, but this is my main job."

"But if you're a deputy chief medical researcher, that means you've graduated with a degree in medicine…?"

"If I were to explain, even briefly, it'd take around twenty minutes. I'll tell you more about myself at some other opportunity. Don't you have other questions?"

Ryuunosuke immediately thought of Rinne.

*   *   *

"That girl... Is she okay?"

Ranko nodded.

"Yes. She's still asleep, but her vitals aren't anything to be concerned about. I expect her to wake up soon."

"That's good to know..."

Ryuunosuke was overcome with relief.

"Sorry," said Ranko, "I should have thanked you, first of all."

"For what? I haven't done anything, really..."

"On the contrary. The whole country... No, the whole world owes you thanks for your contributions. You not only saved her, but also the entire world."

"I did what...?"

He remembered Rinne saying something along those lines, too, but Ryuunosuke was just a high schooler who didn't feel for a moment that he'd been saving the world. It wasn't as if he'd defused an explosive powerful enough to blow the world to smithereens or defeated a powerful demon lord. He just happened to be there when two very strange girls had their very strange duel.

"Hard as it may be for you to believe, it's true. Accept it or not. So I'm guessing you'd like to check in on Rinne. Let's continue our conversation on the way to her, if you're not too tired to walk."

Ryuunosuke realized there were actually a lot of things he wanted to ask Ranko. He changed into his uniform and followed her out of the sick bay.

The sterile white hallway reminded him of a hospital. They passed by many rooms with closed doors. Security cameras were monitoring everything.

"What actually goes on in this underground research facility?"

"We research mythical girls, investigating their mythical factors and ways to preserve them. We also protect, supervise, or restrain the girls as necessary, also ensuring their special qualities remain a secret from the society at large. The Calamity Research Institute is an independent organization unaffiliated with any particular country and operates outside most laws. To put it simply, this is a secret base of a secret organization."

"'Secret' this, 'secret' that… Okay, and what are these mythical factors and mythical girls you've been talking about? I mean, I get that Abara and the other girl are in this mythical girl category."

"Hmm, how should I explain it to you without making it too complicated for a layperson…?"

Ranko fell silent, thinking, as they continued down the hallway. They passed other people dressed like researchers and a few armed guards.

"First of all, I have to stress that they are human. They are human girls who display characteristics of mythical creatures that do not exist, such as dragon wings or vampire fangs. Those characteristics indicate the presence of a mythical factor. Girls who possess a mythical factor are referred to as mythical girls."

"So…mythical girls are girls with powers of supernatural creatures like dragons or vampires?"

"It's not exactly that, but it's okay for you to understand it that way."

They had to pass through a few doors, which Ranko unlocked with codes.

"When a factor manifests, the affected girl involuntarily gains superhuman and paranormal abilities. You've seen yourself what those girls were capable of."

Ryuunosuke thought about Mari and Rinne's battle. Turning blood into weapons, growing wings to fly, lifting impossibly heavy objects— those certainly were supernatural abilities.

"Are there lots of girls like this, secretly existing in this world next to us oblivious ordinary humans?"

Ranko shook her head.

"As far as we are aware, there are only seven mythical factors, and only one girl with each factor is present at a time. When a mythical girl dies, the factor migrates to another girl, so there are always exactly seven."

Ranko listed the seven factors for Ryuunosuke. "In other words..."

First Factor: Unicorn
Second Factor: Amorphous
Third Factor: Dragon
Fourth Factor: Phoenix
Fifth Factor: Vampire
Sixth Factor: Werewolf
Seventh Factor: Succubus

"...there is a mythical girl out there for every factor, although we haven't been able to locate the phoenix girl in the last decade. Unlike the other factors, the phoenix factor can be dormant for some time."

Ryuunosuke nodded slowly to show he was listening.

"And you're researching girls with these...mythical creature powers—no, factors—here in this facility."

"Yes, although it's to be disputed whether the girls possess powers modeled on mythical creatures, or whether these creatures were invented based on powers observed in these girls."

Ranko flapped her arms with the sleeves dangling below her hands, frustrated at having to explain an apparently very complex idea in very simple terms.

Speaking of vampires...

"President, did you know about Abara? About what she is?"

"Yes, naturally. Both that she is a mythical girl and a member of the Order. I've known this from the day she enrolled at our school. She, too, is aware that I know."

"And what's this 'Order'?"

"Both the Order and the Calamity Research Institute descended from the same original organization. Although we are currently hostile to each other, what they do and what we do is very similar, except their ways are more extreme than ours. They can be trusted to keep the matter of mythical girls confidential, at least."

"Oh boy. I had no idea two of my fellow student council members were involved in crazy stuff like that." He suddenly gasped. "Wait... Don't tell me Isurugi and Owari are also involved in super-secret stuff like this?!"

"No, they are perfectly ordinary students."

"And why did both you and Abara enroll at my school? Don't tell me...I have some special powers you're after?!"

"No, you are a perfectly ordinary... Scratch that, you are a peculiar but still normal student. Nobody was targeting you, although you do have a certain 'power,' which I'll explain later. To Abara, the student identity was probably a useful cover for spying. I enrolled at your school...because I thought it'd be fun. And it was the closest to my house."

"'Fun,' huh..."

Ryuunosuke was sure Ranko was hiding something, but he knew her well enough not to probe that topic.

"What's going to happen to Abara? Will she be arrested...?"

"If only it were that easy. The authorities won't do anything. Or to be precise, they *can't* do anything. I don't know what the Order might do. If she keeps coming to our school as normal, I'd like to keep our relationship the same as before. We may belong to opposing organizations, but I have nothing against her personally."

Ranko stopped in front of a door. Unlike the automatic doors they'd passed through before, this one was bigger and reinforced to prevent anyone without authorization from getting in...or out. She unlocked it, and they entered the room.

The space was large and quite dark. At the center was a faintly glowing, semitransparent box—a prison cell equipped with a shower and a toilet. It granted no privacy at all. And the cell had an inmate.

"There she is..."

Rinne Irako, the girl with the dragon factor, was inside.

"This is Rinne Irako, the mythical girl possessing the Third Factor, the dragon. Her code name is Dragon Princess. She was at berserk phase one when you soul linked with her."

Rinne was dressed in a straitjacket like when he first saw her, but she didn't have a tail or wings. She was tied to a chair, still asleep. Her sleeping face looked so innocent, it seemed impossible that she was the same dragon girl who'd fought so fiercely earlier that night.

"She was going to be executed."

Ranko looked at Rinne in the box, but the researcher seemed to be seeing some place far away.

"What?"

Ryuunosuke thought he'd misheard.

"All the mythical factors have the devil inside them."

"The...devil?"

"The proper name is *Heimdall, the End-Bringer Factor.* Existing on the astral plane, this factor awakens with each appearance of a mythical factor, growing and gaining sentience parallel to it. You can think of it as a spiritual cancer. I'm not joking about it becoming sentient. You've seen the mark on Rinne's breast?"

Ryuunosuke had a flashback to when Rinne exposed her chest.

"Er... I wouldn't say it was on her breast... It was on her torso, below the neck..."

"That was a Stigma. The devil inside her. Allowed to grow, it would eventually overtake her mind and body and manifest in our world. We measure the degree of its growth by what we call the berserk phase. You've seen it."

"But she wasn't going berserk, losing her mind and attacking everyone around."

"Because she was only at berserk phase one. At that phase, she was still able to think clearly but couldn't switch between expressing and disabling her mythical creature abilities and characteristics. In other words, she couldn't hide her tail and wings, for example."

That checked out—Rinne had her tail and wings out from the time Ryuunosuke met her until she'd fallen asleep.

"At berserk phase two, the devil's consciousness comes to the surface. At the final phase, a berserk mythical girl begins to lay waste to everything around, causing cataclysmal destruction. What happens depends on the factor involved. In the case of the dragon factor, it's fairly straightforward—the dragon heart overheats, turning the mythical girl into a bomb. Rinne's destructive potential is rated highest."

"This rating means nothing to me, though. How much damage are we talking?"

"Do you know about the Tunguska event in 1908? A huge explosion near the Podkamennaya Tunguska River in Russia?"

"Er... Sorry, I'm not particularly good at world history..."

"Well, suffice it to say, it was an explosion on monstrous scale. An area the size of Tokyo was totally destroyed."

"What? An area the size of Tokyo?"

"It happened in a remote area, so there were only a few casualties. The explosion was attributed to a meteor. At least, that's the official version of the events."

"But that's not what really happened...?"

"No. The explosion was caused by the overheating of a berserk dragon girl's heart. The annals of history are peppered with such large-scale destructive events that were, unbeknownst to the public, caused by mythical girls. Anyway, the Tunguska event was rated third for its destructiveness. Top-rated damage equals the destruction of modern civilizations. To the Calamity Research Institute, that is synonymous with the destruction of the world. That is the scale of explosion Rinne could cause if she went berserk."

"...I'm surprised the world hasn't been destroyed yet by one of these mythical girls."

"It has come close to total destruction, but the disasters were prevented just in time by executing mythical girls who showed signs of going berserk or had already lost control. The growth of the devil in them can be slowed with special medication, but it cannot be completely stopped. From the moment a mythical girl obtains the factor powers, she's set on a path to her execution."

"That's brutal..."

"..."

Ranko looked sadly at Rinne in the cell.

"Er… And what happens to the mythical girls when they're executed?"

"What do you think? They die, like any human. The only difference is that the mythical factor they had been hosting migrates to another girl's soul. Another girl becomes a mythical girl. After she dies, the factor will migrate yet again. And so on."

"Hold on," Ryuunosuke interrupted. "At berserk phase one, the factor characteristics show all the time. That's what you said, right? But when I touched Rinne's— What was it again? Right, Stigma. When I touched it, a light appeared on my left hand—it's gone now, and I just have this dark mark, but it was a bright light at the time—so when that light appeared, Rinne's horns disappeared. What's that mean?"

"We're getting to the most important part now. That ring you have is known as a Sacred Sealing Ring. Those who possess them are called soul linkers."

"I'm a…soul linker?"

"Contact with the mythical girl was presumably the trigger. The moment you touched Rinne, your link activated, and the Sacred Sealing Ring appeared. The fact that you were there at that time was nothing short of a miracle."

Ryuunosuke traced the ring mark with his right index finger.

"I'm sorry that all I can tell you is my hypothesis of what occurred. This field has been poorly researched, and there are few historical records of soul linkers and Sacred Sealing Rings. It probably will be a while before we discover why you have this power or why Sacred Sealing Rings exist in the first place. But it is certain that your miraculous appearance when Rinne needed you diametrically changed her situation."

Ranko began walking toward the prison cell in the middle of the room. Ryuunosuke followed.

"Sacred Sealing Rings have the power to absorb mythical girls' sins, control their devils, and rule over all factors. Their most impressive ability is to stop a mythical girl from going berserk. When a soul linker touches a mythical girl's Stigma and makes the soul wedding vows, their souls become linked."

"Hold on... Did you say 'soul wedding'...?"

When Rinne asked him to wed her, he thought she meant marriage. It wouldn't have ever occurred to him that she was talking about something occult. The vows she'd made sounded just like what people said during wedding ceremonies.

"Soul linking strengthens the factor, stops the growth of the devil within, and cancels the berserk status."

"So that's why Rinne's fine now."

Ranko nodded.

"Also, some of the factor's abilities are fed back to the linker. Your arm injury was healed thanks to the dragon factor's regenerative ability. Linkers don't benefit from the full power of the factor, though, which is why you have a scar left. A critical injury would kill you. Dragon powers can only do so much when you're an ordinary human."

"I see..."

"However, if soul linking is capable of enhancing a factor's power and stopping it from going berserk, it might also be possible for it to have the opposite effect."

"What do you mean?"

"Soul unlinking might elevate the berserk phase and weaken the factor. It is just my untested theory, of course, but I believe it's now within your power to end this world if you harbor nihilistic inclinations."

"N-no, I don't!"

"It was just a joke, I know you wouldn't do such a thing. By the way, nobody has ever managed to restore a mythical girl's control once she reached berserk phase two. Soul linking requires the girl's consent, which she'd be unable to give after losing her senses."

"Meaning rings have to be used before the berserk phase gets too advanced, or it's game over."

"Yes. I have been researching the production of synthetic Sacred Sealing Rings to free mythical girls from their curse, but so far, I've had no results. This is about to change, though. Now that I have access to authentic rings, I'm confident I can finally make headway with that project. In all honesty, I would love for you to soul link with every mythical girl out there, but we don't know what effect that might have on you. There are too many uncertainties. We must be very cautious about how we go about this."

Ranko put her hand on the wall of Rinne's prison.

"Dazai boy, will you team up with me to prevent more girls from ending up like her?"

"You want me to work with you?"

"With your ring, you can help not only Rinne, but also all the other mythical girls. It wouldn't be an exaggeration to say you'd be saving the world. Also, I wouldn't want my research on you to be interrupted by the Order. I want to keep you close, for personal reasons."

Ranko offered him her hand.

"Well? Won't you use your power to help us?"

"My 'power'..."

"I've been researching Sacred Sealing Rings and soul linkers for a very long time. Having a real soul linker right here is like a dream come true, not just for me but for the mythical girls, too. You're our paragon of hope—a savior."

"Me, a savior..."

"The Order will be desperate to have you in their hands, as well. They will fight to get you. Your life won't return to how it used to be anyway, and many dangers await you. I will ask you one last time. Please help us."

Ryuunosuke looked at the confined dragon girl.

"I don't really know how much I'll be able to help..."

The truth was, he'd already made up his mind even before Ranko listed all the reasons he should help her.

"...but I'll do what I can."

He shook Ranko's hand with conviction.

"Thank you, and sorry in advance for involving you in this."

"No need to apologize. I'd gladly do anything you ask, President— you know that. So what do we do now?"

"It's quite simple, really. From now on, you and Rinne will—"

◆

"Huh?!"

Ryuunosuke woke with a gasp. He was lying on a tatami floor. On the low ceiling above was a familiar lamp. He looked around at the slightly grimy walls and sliding door. He was, without doubt, back home in his seven-by-five tatami room, which was strewed with dumbbells and karate paraphernalia. There was a tiny bathroom and a separate tiny toilet room. The floors creaked when you walked on them.

The furniture was basic, and it was old, cheaply made, or old *and* cheaply made. The house was an okay size for one person, but for two, it'd be quite cramped. It was a rental one-story house built several decades ago, with a wooden roof and rusty-red walls made of corrugated iron. It was Ryuunosuke's home.

"It was just a dream..."

The sunlight shining through the window made him squint, and he thought about that strange dream. He rubbed out the tatami mat impression on his cheek. He was feeling dazed and sluggish.

"Ow... That hurts..."

His whole body felt stiff and sore. For some reason, he was wearing a crisp white shirt that looked brand-new. It was sticking to his sweaty skin.

"I need a bath..."

He'd only just woken up, but he felt dog-tired. Unsteadily, he made his way to the changing room. It was only a few steps, since his house was so small.

Ryuunosuke opened the door to the changing room. He lived alone and never had guests over. But he was in for a surprise.

"Excuse me?"

"Eep!"

There was a girl in his changing room. Her long hair was wet, as was the rest of her delicate, fair-skinned body, which was flushed from the hot water. He'd walked in on her when she was toweling off. She was no stranger—it was none other than Rinne Irako.

Ryuunosuke's mind froze, unable to process the situation. A new flush appeared on Rinne's face as she glared at him.

*   *   *

"You are wed to me, but in your eagerness, do not act like a tactless oaf!"

She slammed the door shut on him.

"…"

Ryuunosuke stared at the closed changing room door blankly.

"You're up, Dazai boy? Good morning."

Someone tapped his shoulder. Ryuunosuke turned and saw a listless girl in a lab coat that was a few sizes too big for her—Ranko Akeda.

"Huh…? President? What are you doing in my house?"

"I understand you are a healthy young man with rampaging hormones, but peeping on a girl taking a bath is really rude."

"I wasn't peeping on her! But wait, nothing is making any sense…"

"Not to hurry you, but you should get ready for school," Ranko said, heading toward his room as if it was the most natural thing to do.

Ryuunosuke stopped her.

"Can you explain just what on earth is going on?"

"Hmm? Ah, yes, your memory must not be functioning properly yet. It's a side effect of hypnosis. Don't worry, you'll remember everything soon enough," she replied, going into his room.

The haze in Ryuunosuke's head gradually cleared, and he finally remembered what Ranko had told him just before he'd lost consciousness.

"From now on, you and Rinne will be living together."

CHAPTER 3

Dragon Pandemonium at School

Project Code Name: Dragon Babysitter.

"I would like you to join the Dragon Babysitter Project in a support role," Ranko had said to Ryuunosuke before he passed out. *"As a soul linker, you are an extremely valuable resource to the Calamity Research Institute. The Order will want you just as much. By living together with Rinne, you will be able to react to the slightest signs of her going berserk and stop it, and she will keep you safe from the Order. If the ring's effect is enhanced by your proximity, it's best for you two to stick close."*

The Dragon Babysitter Project involved monitoring the berserk-suppressing effects of the ring over time, with the end goal being the permanent eradication of the mythical factor.

"By the way, I'll also be moving in with you, as emergency medical support and project supervisor."

"What? I'll have you living in my house, too?"

"Why are you giving me attitude? Don't want me as a roommate? I saw it; I saw you cringe just now. You've made me so sad. My feelings are irreparably hurt. And here I thought we were friends."

"Don't put words in my mouth. I never said anything about not wanting you to move in!"

Immediately after that, she shone that strange light into his eyes again, and he woke up in his house.

"Right, I remember our conversation now, and everything that led up to it... But am I seriously sharing the place with two girls? My house is too small for so many people..."

The inventor and supervisor of the Dragon Babysitter Project, Ranko, went to the bathroom to have a shower after Rinne came out.

The amenities in Ryuunosuke's house were all quite old, and it was a tricky job to get the shower temperature right. Rinne must have washed herself in pretty hot water, because as soon as Ranko turned the tap on, she screamed.

With Ranko in the bathroom, the living room became quiet. Rinne's prickly aura was putting Ryuunosuke off from starting a conversation with her.

This is so awkward...

Ryuunosuke—now changed into his school uniform—was pacing around the living room, unnerved by the silence. He glanced over at Rinne, who was sitting at the low dining table.

I'm just not good at speaking with girls... It's different with the student council; we can talk about our tasks, but what can I talk about with others? I've no idea what girls even think about.

Rinne was sitting on her knees, her back straight. She was also dressed in the West Kokonoe High uniform.

She's actually really cute... No, she's a beauty.

Rinne Irako was a strange girl. With mannerisms as dignified as if she were a knight or a samurai, she had an air of mystery around her. When she was beginning to go berserk, her beauty was ephemeral and dangerous, like a melting icicle. Calm like this, she was as adorable as a vanilla ice-cream *manjuu*. Her mysterious beauty was enhanced further by the neatness of the school uniform.

Her straight and proper posture at the table was enough to make the atmosphere in the small room formal.

"Ryuunosuke."

"Bwah?!"

His voice betrayed him. He wasn't prepared to be spoken to.

"Your anxious fidgeting is irritating. Sit down."

"Huh? Oh…"

"Sit down."

"S-sure…"

Unable to resist her commanding tone, he sat down opposite her at the table.

She looks so different from when she was duking it out yesterday…

Rinne didn't have horns or a tail. It seemed unthinkable that this girl had been brutally fighting just the day before, shooting light beams and all that.

Ryuunosuke thought about how he'd found himself in this bizarre situation—suddenly having two pretty girls as roommates—but flustered as he was, he accepted this new reality as something he'd agreed to for a good cause. He couldn't go back on his word.

He did worry about Rinne, though. While it was necessary for him and Rinne to stick together, cohabitating with a dude like him might be stressful for her. He'd have to be very careful to treat her with consideration and not make her uncomfortable.

"…"

He furtively shot her another glance. In contrast, she didn't seem the least bit bothered by the room-sharing. She barely seemed to notice him at all. Her callous and prickly attitude made Ryuunosuke wonder if she hated him. He couldn't blame her if she did after he accidentally walked in on her naked in the changing room.

He gathered up his courage to talk to her.

"So, Irako…"

"Call me Rinne," she said quietly, but with insistence. "We are a wed couple, Ryuunosuke."

"You mean, we're soul linked…"

"Call me by my first name without reserve."

Ryuunosuke cleared his throat.

"Ahem… All right, Ms. Rinne it is."

She looked at him sharply.

"No 'Miss.' Just Rinne."

"Rinne… I wanted to ask you…are you really okay with living with me? Doesn't it bother you? Because if you don't like this, you should say so. Never mind that it's part of this project. It's better for both of us to be honest instead of putting up with something we don't want. I can convince President to—"

"No." She shook her head slightly. "I do not mind."

"Don't worry about hurting my feelings or anything. It must be unpleasant for a young girl to be forced to live with a guy she barely knows. Especially in a small house like mine."

"Listen, Ryuunosuke."

"Y-yes?"

"I chose this. And the reason…is not because we are now bound together by your vows. It is because…"

She shook her head, as if fighting with herself over whether to tell him the reason or not. Her expression didn't visibly change, but Ryuunosuke sensed she was feeling embarrassed.

"Have I done something…?"

"I…," Rinne continued, having made up her mind to be frank with him.

"Yes…?" he encouraged her on.

Rinne looked away from him, her cheeks reddened.

"I love you."

Ryuunosuke crossed his arms, trying to process if he'd really just received a love confession.

"Hmmmmmmmmmm…"

He cocked his head, thinking deeply about what Rinne might mean, because it surely couldn't have been a love confession. They'd only met the previous night. She wouldn't have fallen in love with him so fast. He reasoned that he must have misunderstood her.

"Er… Sorry, I don't see why you'd feel like this about me… Oh, wait. Did you mean 'love' as in 'like a lot,' as a friend?"

"No, I meant that I love you as a person of the opposite sex. As a man. I have romantic feelings for you, or so I believe. It is confusing for me, too, since I have never been in love before. The feelings arose last night, when you saved me, risking your own life. I am certain that I am not mistaking gratitude for love."

"But wait, falling in love with me just because I saved you is—"

"It is what happened. I do not care if you accept my love, and neither am I interested in knowing how you feel about me. I simply put my feelings into words so that you would know that I am not in the least discomforted by the project. Living together is what I would have wished for. I wanted you to know this, but let us drop this subject. It is embarrassing to talk about it further."

Rinne took a deep breath after saying all that in one go, and she turned her flushed face away from him.

Ryuunosuke had been under the impression that Rinne was the quiet type, so her machine-gun monologue was both surprising and overwhelming for him.

"Wh-why are you not saying anything?! A smile or any other sign of happiness would be welcome! Or perhaps..." Rinne's voice grew quieter, and uncertainty appeared in her eyes. "Do you think me not good enough for you?"

"What...? No, of course not..."

"Well, now that we have cleared that up," she said, evidently relieved that he didn't seem to have anything against her. "Thank you for inviting me, an undeserving dragon girl who might end up destroying the world, into your life."

She bowed gracefully to him, touching the tatami mat with her fingertips.

"Uh... Um... The pleasure's mine..."

He was flattered but also embarrassed, so he looked away from her at the grubby low ceiling.

"Well, you know... How to put it...? I bet lots of guys would pay a fortune to swap with me and share the roof with a cute girl like you."

"C-cute...?!"

Ryuunosuke regretted saying that and worried she'd imagine he had dirty intentions toward her. He looked at her with concern...

"...?!"

...and froze with his eyes open wide.

"I—I had never have thought of myself that way... Although, I will agree that my appearance is not unappealing..."

Rinne was blushing, covering her cheeks with her hands bashfully. But that wasn't what had surprised Ryuunosuke.

"Um... Rinne..."

"Yes?"

He pointed at her head.

"Your horns are out."

"Huh?!"

She frantically reached up to touch her head, then felt the two horns.

"Eek?!"

She covered her horns with her hands and hid her head under the table.

"My apologies... It does happen rarely, when I am under the influence of strong emotions..."

"Well, watch out when you're at school. But why are you hiding from me now?"

"I do not wish you, the man my heart has chosen, to see me in that ugly form..."

"You think your horns are ugly?"

"Do you not...find it repulsive that a girl has horns and a tail...?"

"What? Not at all! I think they look really cool."

He didn't say that just to make her feel better. He honestly thought her dragon parts were awesome.

"'Cool'...?"

She peeked out shyly from under the table.

"The first time I saw you, it was a bit of a shock, but what's more awesome than a cute girl with dragon horns and a tail? Boys are suckers for all things dragon, like sew-on dragon patches on their schoolbags and stuff like that."

"Is that so?"

"Absolutely!"

"You seem sincere… So my dragon features do not disgust you?"

"No, I love them!"

"You…love them… I see… Tee-hee… Tee-hee-hee…"

She smiled, wiping a little tear from the corners of her eyes.

It finally hit Ryuunosuke that Rinne felt inferior because of how she looked. He could understand why. Complexes about one's appearance were so widespread in society, and Rinne had features no normal human had. As an adolescent girl, she was very conscious about her body.

"You have strange tastes."

"I wouldn't mind examining your dragon features in more detail sometime. Ha-ha, just kiddin—"

"I will show you now," she said and proceeded to take off her blazer.

"Wh-what? Now?!" Ryuunosuke protested without thinking, shocked at her sudden undressing.

"What is the matter? You were just saying that you wished to see my tail and wings."

"I was just joking… Besides, you don't need to undress for that…"

"I do need to do that, or else my uniform will tear. I would rather not destroy my new clothes… Unless you wish to see them ripped to pieces when I transform?"

Her mythical-creature body parts grew as an extension of her own body when she transformed, so of course, she'd wreck any clothes she was wearing.

"Er… No, I don't want you to destroy your clothes! Just take them off. No, wait, what am I saying, don't, it was a joke—"

"I understand. You are disgusted by me after all…"

She looked at him with hurt like an abandoned puppy. Ryuunosuke couldn't bear it.

"Argh… I mean, I said it as a joke, but now I can't wait to see your dragon parts!" he bellowed.

"You are hard work, Ryuunosuke. If you are so keen to see me, I will do my best to please you."

She energetically resumed undressing. She folded her blazer and put it on the floor next to her. Next, she removed the ribbon around her neck. Then she started unfastening the buttons of her blouse. She looked so sexy doing that, Ryuunosuke had to avert his gaze. It was ironic that he was acting prudish after telling her to undress in front of him.

Rinne took off her blouse, remaining in her bra. The straps left an opening on her back, leaving space for her dragon wings.

When Rinne reached for the hooks fastening her skirt, Ryuunosuke stopped her.

"Sorry, do you mind keeping your skirt on?"

"As you wish."

He said that to stop her from exposing her panties, but it ended up sounding as if he was a perv with a skirt fetish.

And so Rinne was sitting on the floor opposite her pervy, fetishistic roommate, her upper body naked but for the bra.

"Could I... Could I ask you to close your eyes for a moment? I would not yet feel comfortable being seen while I am transforming."

"Oh, okay."

Ryuunosuke closed his eyes. He actually wanted to see her transformation sequence, but he had to respect her wishes. Showing someone parts that were normally kept hidden could be embarrassing, so that made sense... Ryuunosuke thought she should've asked him to close his eyes when she was taking her clothes off, too, but he didn't say anything, being the guilty party here.

He heard noises like joints creaking and really wanted to open his eyes, but he fought his curiosity.

"I...I am ready now. You may look."

Ryuunosuke waited just a moment longer before opening his eyes. In front of him was a beautiful girl in a skirt and a bra. Crucially, she now possessed extra body parts—dragon horns, wings, and a tail. Just like the other night.

"Oooh..."

Despite having seen her like that before, he couldn't help gasping in awe.

"Well…? Say something."

"Sorry, it's just so amazing, I was speechless…"

"Really…? I am pleased that you like what you see."

"That's good…"

"Would you like to…touch them?"

"Yeah… Huh, for real?!"

Ryuunosuke was totally bewildered by her offer. He was feeling terribly shy, and also guilty for having started this. Touching a girl's body was something entirely new to him. But he was incredibly curious about the dragon parts, and he had to be brave and help Rinne overcome her complexes. Curiosity won in the end.

"Are you sure you're okay with me touching them?"

"The admiration in your eyes convinced me. I will allow it as a special favor for you only, Ryuunosuke."

"I see, thanks…"

He sat down next to Rinne, noticing she was being bashful.

"All right, then. I'm going to touch you…"

"Please proceed. I…g-grant you my permission…"

Ryuunosuke picked up her thick tail and put it over his knees.

"Wow, so this is what a dragon tail feels like. It's heavy. Reminds me of the python I held once at a zoo a long time ago. And you can move it?"

"Y-yes, of course…"

She wiggled her tail in a snakelike motion. It was strong, and Ryuunosuke felt as if he was holding a large, very lively fish. He rubbed the tip of her tail, curious about the texture.

"Mngh…," Rinne moaned softly, shifting her position.

Ryuunosuke touched her tail until his curiosity was satisfied. Next, he turned his attention to her wings and horns, putting his hands on them without inhibition. Rinne wriggled slightly whenever he stroked her wings or the tips of her horns, but Ryuunosuke didn't notice.

"Do you have inverted scales on your neck? And does touching them make you furious, like in the legends? Inverted dragon scales are rare items in some games, you know?"

He reached for her neck.

"N-no, stop. Do not touch me there…!"

Ryuunosuke tried to give her a little scratch on the neck, as you would with a dog or a cat, but no sooner had his fingers grazed her than Rinne shoved him away.

"Ouchie!"

Ryuunosuke fell onto his back. When he sat up, he saw that Rinne's dragon parts had disappeared, and she was putting her blouse back on. Her hands were shaking so much, she couldn't do the buttons, so she gave up, leaving the blouse open. She turned to look at Ryuunosuke, breathing heavily.

"Um, Rinne? Are you angry with me? You didn't like me touching you?"

Rinne grabbed him by the shoulders. Her cheeks were flushed, there were beads of perspiration on her forehead, and she was panting.

"My apologies. I had to reabsorb my dragon features so as not to accidentally injure you with my horns."

"Ow, you're squeezing too tight—it hurts… What's wrong…?"

She pushed him down onto the floor and sat on top of him, pinning his arms to the ground with her legs.

"Whoa?! What are you doing? I'm sorry if I did something bad!"

"You have done a very bad thing. Touching the inverted scales on my neck when I am in my dragon form sends me into this feverish state. I am feeling a little frisky."

"You mean 'furious,' right?!"

"I assure you I am not at all upset with you."

"But what the heck? I really can't move! You're too strong! Dragon power is badass! You don't need your horns out to have superhuman strength?!"

Rinne's weight was perfectly average for a girl her age, and her build was petite, not athletic. And yet no matter how hard Ryuunosuke struggled to free himself, he couldn't move at all.

Rinne bent over to whisper in his ear. Her long hair tickled his face, and a sweet smell enveloped him. He could see her full, glossy lips parting out of the corner of his eye.

"It is my turn now."

Her whisper was clear and spellbindingly alluring.

"You have touched my body, so it stands to reason that I should have the opportunity to touch yours, too, would you not agree?"

"Touch WHAT?!"

She began to deftly unbutton his shirt with one hand.

"Do not worry, it will not hurt. Men enjoy this, Ranko told me. Count the stains on your ceiling to distract yourself, and it will soon be over..."

"What in the world has Ranko been teaching you?!"

Rinne began tracing a shape on his chest with her dainty index finger. Ryuunosuke thought for a moment that little heart shapes appeared in her eyes.

"I'd like to take things a little slower, please!!!"

"Oh, do not be such a baby. Stop resisting and let me ravage you already."

"Aaaaaargh! H-heeelp! President! Dr. Akedaaa!"

Right after he called her, Ranko came back from the bathroom.

"Why are you kicking up such a fuss so early in the morning?"

She was naked.

"Put your clothes on!"

"You're not making any sense. It was you who called me. I hurried to see what the problem was, and you yell at me?"

"Argh, forget it! If you could just help me, that'd be great!"

"Rinne, what are you doing to him?"

"Ryuunosuke said he wanted to touch my tail and horns, and I complied. Yet he went further and touched my inverse scales, so now I am in the middle of satisfying my own urge to touch his body."

"It was your idea, Rinne! You offered to let me touch you!"

"You be quiet!"

"Hmm..." Ranko stroked her chin, thinking. "The moral of the story is: You reap what you sow. Everybody knows that you do not touch the inverse scales of a dragon."

"Does everyone know that?!"

Rinne pinned him down even harder, and it was clear that he would receive no sympathy from the coldly logical Ranko. The dragon girl reached for the last button of his shirt.

"Whether you want this or not is irrelevant," she said. "It is compulsory. Surrender to my power."

"'Can't stop this violence with reasoning'—is that what you're saying?!"

"You saved me, Ryuunosuke. And you touched my special parts... What are you, if not my mate?"

"'Mate'?!"

"It means one of a pair, or a sexual partner of an animal. Rinne's saying you're basically husband and wife," Ranko piped up.

"I didn't ask you for an interpretation!"

"With a mate possessing such low cognitive powers, I do worry for our future..."

"Even a psychic would be hella confused in this situation!"

"Please calm down. We are a wed couple, and our souls are already linked. Now we only need to link our bodies. We will be skipping a few steps on our way toward bonding, but does that really matter? I do not consider it a problem. We can iron out the kinks later. You can trust me with this—I have crammed the theory into my head."

"Theory of what?! President! Don't just grin and watch—help me! Please help!"

"Everything's going to be okay, Dazai boy. I have taken care of Rinne's you-know-what education, personally selecting the very best books on the subject for her. She knows the theory."

"And what about ethical considerations for the test subject—me?! Also, get dressed already! You'll catch a cold, walking around naked after a bath!"

Suddenly, Ryuunosuke heard someone turn the knob of his front door, and the door opened.

*   *   *

"Ryuu? Is everything okay?"

It was the worst timing ever. A chill ran down Ryuunosuke's spine when he heard that voice. He looked up at the clock on the wall. He always walked to school with Aya Isurugi, his neighbor and childhood friend, but it wasn't yet the time they usually left together.

"What's with all the noise? We could hear you screaming from my house. I brought you something to eat. I know you've been skipping breakfast because you're broke," she called to him from the entrance hall.

That morning had been so crazy, Ryuunosuke had forgotten about Aya. Normally, he'd be over the moon if she brought him breakfast, but that particular morning, he wished she hadn't turned up.

"Stop, Isurugi! Don't come into the living room!"

"What? What's going on with you today, Ryuu…? Oh…"

Aya, in her school uniform and with a reusable shopping bag filled with food, stopped in her tracks right after entering the living room. Let's objectively consider what sight she'd been exposed to. There was the pretty much stark-naked student council president. A young woman she had never seen before was straddling her childhood friend, evidently stripping him of his clothes. And lastly, her childhood friend was lying on his back with his shirt open.

"Er…"

She froze, and who could blame her? As far as she'd known, she was the only girl close to Ryuunosuke, so finding him in the company of one naked and one half-naked girl was quite a shock.

"Eeeeeeeeeeeeeeeek!" she finally squealed in a voice Ryuunosuke had never heard from her before, covering her mouth.

"Oh, it's Isurugi. Hello."

"Another female intrudes on me and the man who has wed me…"

Ryuunosuke felt defeated. All he could do was mitigate the damage that had already been done. He took a deep breath,

"Isurugi, I can explain this."

◆

In the end, Ryuunosuke managed to get Aya to believe him. He told her that Ranko and Rinne were half sisters with different fathers. After remarrying, Ranko's father and their mother worked as researchers at a pharmaceutical company until her untimely death in an accident. Rinne lived with her dad abroad until he died, too, and then she came to Japan to move in with Ranko, but they got kicked out from the apartment Ranko had been renting. With nowhere else to go, they had come to stay at Ryuunosuke's house—he was actually their distant relative. Rinne would be going to West Kokonoe High starting that day. She didn't know much about Japanese customs and social rules, because she had spent a long time in a hospital abroad due to a medical condition. The scene Aya had witnessed was just the result of a cultural misunderstanding—that was all.

That's what Ryuunosuke told Aya. It was all made-up, of course, but that was the "official" background story they'd be going with. Except that he hadn't had the time to brief Rinne about it, which predictably led to problems. While he was desperately trying to sell the story to Aya, quickly stringing ideas together, Rinne would suddenly say something weird, and he had no idea if she was doing that on purpose to make it difficult for him or if she was just being slow. Aya would then question him, and he'd brush it off somehow. Ranko stayed out of the conversation, as if it didn't concern her.

"Ryuunosuke is my mate."

"Y-your what?! Ryuu, what is she talking about?!"

"Rinne, you're phrasing it in a way that invites misunderstandings!"

"He has wed me."

"Wed you?! Ryuu, what is she talking about?!"

"Rinne, you're doing this again—wrong phrasing!"

"By the way, Ryuunosuke, I am getting hungry."

"She's hungry? Ryuu, what is she talking about?!"

"She's just hungry! This, for once, isn't anything weird!"

It was grueling, but eventually, Ryuunosuke convinced Aya that nothing untoward had been going on in his house. The reason for Ranko's nakedness wasn't stated, but then again, Aya didn't ask.

Once the situation calmed down, Aya put together breakfast, and all four of them ate together. Aya's first impression of Rinne wasn't great, and at first, there was some awkwardness between them, but soon enough, they warmed up to each other. Aya had a caring personality and always saw the best in people, so she made friends quickly.

"Okay, we're going now," Ryuunosuke called to Ranko from the entrance hall.

Ranko was skipping school that day to take care of something at home, she said. Ryuunosuke guessed she would be busy with her research work.

"Have a good day," Ranko replied, walking to the front door to see the three of them off.

Nobody noticed the complex mix of emotions in her eyes as she looked at Rinne getting ready to go to school, dressed in her uniform again.

"Rinne," she said just as the girl started walking away.

Rinne turned and waited. After a brief pause, Ranko said to her, "Have fun."

"I shall!"

Rinne nodded with determination. She had never been to school before.

"School will be something new for me. I shall make the most of it."

It didn't show on her face, but Ryuunosuke sensed she'd been filled with anticipation since morning.

"You didn't go to school where you lived before?" he asked.

"No. But I had received standard education at the facility."

"No way, you've never been to a school before?!"

Ryuunosuke suddenly regretted touching that topic when Aya was around.

"Er... Her, um, her situation's been pretty unusual..."

"Ah, her medical condition..."

Aya looked so sad thinking about it. Ryuunosuke thought she was a really good person, and he felt like crap for having to lie to her.

"Hurry, or I will leave you behind!" Rinne called out.

"What? You don't even know the way!"

School would be an entirely new experience for Rinne, and she must have been terribly excited about it. She started running with a spring in her steps, like a happy little girl, toward an intersection with poor visibility, warning signs about children crossing, and school-zone markings painted on the asphalt.

"Don't run on the road—it's dangerous."

"I am not a child, Ryuunosuke. I know how to keep saf—"

Her voice was drowned out by the screech of a truck braking suddenly, the tires rubbing against the asphalt. The ground shook as the truck collided with Rinne. A truck going sixty kilometers per hour hitting a girl weighing maybe forty-five kilograms could only have one result. Even a preschooler would have no doubts as to what would happen. It came down to the simple laws of physics.

Ryuunosuke froze in horror. Blood drained from his face, which tensed almost painfully, and his balls retreated upward.

It's my fault... The truck... Reincarnation... Is the driver okay? It's my fault... It's an accident... What will I say to President...? It's my fault...

Jumbled thoughts were racing in his head. He didn't want to see the gruesome aftermath of the collision...

"I... I did not see you coming..."

...and he didn't, because there wasn't much to see, except for a rather surprised Rinne standing with one hand braced against the front of the truck. Mythical girls were an exception to rules that bound ordinary humans.

The front of the truck was caved in, and the surface of the road was cracked and broken like an ice sheet under Rinne's feet. Her uniform had gotten a little dusty, but otherwise, she was perfectly fine.

Rinne's cute looks made Ryuunosuke forget that she had abilities surpassing any other extant life-form. Even if the truck had hit her head-on, she'd probably be fine.

The truck driver was still in his seat, absolutely petrified. A crowd of onlookers began to gather, attracted by the sound of the crash.

"What is it?"

"Was there an accident?"

"Has anyone... Has anyone called for an ambulance yet? And the police?"

It was the peak of the morning commute. There were lots of people around, and an incident like that was bound to attract attention.

"Um, Ryuu... Is it just me, or did Rinne stop the truck with her han—?"

"What? No, no! The truck stopped just in time! Thank goodness for that! Rinne, I told you to be careful on the road! Ha-ha... Ha-ha... Ha-ha-ha-ha!"

The driver seemed unhurt, but just in case, Ryuunosuke took a mental note of the number plate and the company name written on the side to report to Ranko later. He then put one arm around Rinne and another around Aya, then quickly ran from the scene.

◆

Ryuunosuke and Aya gave Rinne a thorough tour of the school before stopping at the teachers' room, and then they headed to their classroom without Rinne. Rinne was in the same class as them, 2-B, but first, she had to go meet her homeroom teacher on her own.

Ryuunosuke sat down in his seat and rested his cheek in his hand. He had gone to Mari's classroom to check on her, but she wasn't there.

What was I expecting...?

Like Ranko, Mari was only posing as a student. Now that the Order's plan to capture Rinne had failed and, to make matters worse, Ryuunosuke found out about Mari's true identity, she probably had no reason to return to the school. As a member of the Dragon Babysitter Project, Ryuunosuke was Mari's enemy, but it didn't feel like that to him. He still thought of her as his fellow student council member and his junior. It made him a bit sad to think he might never see her again.

"She didn't have any hard feelings, I think... She's not a bad person," he muttered to himself.

He wanted to soul link with her, too, to stop her from going berserk someday, but Ranko had told him to hold off until she made more progress with the Sacred Sealing Ring research. But then again, he wouldn't be able to link with Mari anyway if she stopped coming to school. He had no way of finding her.

He idly tuned in to a random conversation his ears picked out from the surrounding chatter.

"Oh, Yukachi, did you hear that a transfer student is joining our class?"

"Really? Hey, that's new. Are they a looker? Girl or boy?"

"I don't know, I just heard Micchan talking about a transfer student."

The girls were referring to Rinne.

People already know about her joining our class? She was only enrolled a day ago... No, less than that. Normally, you wouldn't be able to transfer to a new school in just a day... President must have pulled some strings. I guess she has some authority over the school. Poor teacher, having to deal with a sudden change like that... The Calamity Research Institute works fast, getting Rinne a uniform in her size in such a short time.

The Calamity Research Institute was a secret organization covering up phenomena like UFO or cryptid incidents from the public, though. Enrolling a new student in a public school in less than a day must have been easy for them.

The homeroom chime sounded briefly, and the homeroom teacher came into the classroom. The teacher, a woman around thirty years old who always looked tired, seemed even more beat that day.

"Hello, I have some unexpected news... Unexpected not just for you guys… So it seems we've got a transfer student who'll be with us starting from today."

An excited murmur rippled through the class.

"Please come in, Irako."

The classroom door opened.

I wonder if Rinne's going to be nervous. It'd be kind of funny to see her panic. Nah… She's the type to say, "Be grateful you get to have me in your class!" But maybe she'll just go with the standard "Hello. I'm Rinne Irako. Nice to meet you," and play it cool…

Ryuunosuke waited, still resting his cheek in his hand. At last, she entered the room. Her face was as neutral as usual. She walked oddly, though, as if on stilts.

Total stage fright!

She was clearly very tense. Her neutral face wasn't nonchalant; it was hiding fear. Her eyes were wide, her mouth was pressed into a tight line, and her fingers quivered. Actually, she was shaking all over.

Ryuunosuke thought she looked more like a baby bunny thrown into a carnivorous animal's cage than a dragon.

"Irako? Um, no need to be scared…" The teacher tried to encourage her.

"Eep!" Rinne squeaked, startled.

"Will you tell everyone your name…? It's okay if you just write it on the blackboard. Irako has been living abroad for a long time. Please keep in mind that everything is very new for her here."

Rinne wrote her name on the blackboard horizontally in neat characters, but they were of uneven size, with the first two characters very big and the rest getting smaller and smaller.

It was Rinne's first day in a school, and probably also her first time being surrounded by so many other teenagers. Of course she'd be nervous.

"M-m-my…," she stuttered, too anxious to speak, maybe forgetting what she was about to say.

At that point, Rinne seemed about to cry. She was wringing her hands, looking down at the floor. Seeing her like that stirred Ryuunosuke's protective instincts.

You can do it!

He was sending encouraging vibes her way, and he wasn't the only one. He could sense that all the other students in the classroom were also focused on Rinne, watching her with bated breaths. In their hearts, they were all wishing for her to find the courage.

"M-my name is Rinne Irako. I have lived abroad for many years, so everything here is very unfamiliar to me. I hope I do not do anything to upset anyone. It is nice to meet you."

Nobody tried to make fun of her while she was introducing herself. Everyone listened in silence until she was finished, and then everyone stood up, unprompted by the teacher, to applaud Rinne. If someone peered into the classroom from the hallway, they'd be confused by the scene, but what mattered was that Rinne received the warmest of welcomes.

◆

After Rinne's introduction to the class, the teacher made a few short announcements.

Rinne took a desk at the back, near the windows. It was diagonally across from Ryuunosuke's. Since her arrival was unplanned, the desk order had changed a little, but nobody minded. Other girls crowded around Rinne's desk, asking her lots of questions.

"I hope she's going to be okay…and that she doesn't blurt out anything she shouldn't," Ryuunosuke muttered.

"Well, look at her! Already part of the group, from the looks of it."

"That's good on one hand, but…," the person next to him said reassuringly.

"She's not as good at pretending to be a sweet ordinary girl as me, is she?"

"She's grown up more sheltered than you, Abara... Wait... Abara...?"

Ryuunosuke turned. The mythical vampire girl, Mari Abara, was standing right next to him.

"Whaaat?!"

Completely caught off guard, he stood from his chair and retreated until his back was pressed against the lockers.

"A pretty girl comes to talk to you, and you shriek like you've seen a ghost?"

"Wh-wh-wh-why are you here?!"

"Why? I'm a student at this school. Where else should I be? Don't tell me you've been worried about not seeing me again? Aw, Ryuunosuke Dazai. Silly you!"

Her flirty tone reminded him of a manga dialogue bubble with heart symbols at the end of each sentence. She poked his side, as playful as always.

"B-but... Last night..."

"Ah yes, I was going to talk to you about it."

"Y-you were?"

"Yes. I wanted to say I'm sorry about what happened."

She looked at him with a gentleness she didn't usually display.

"It's okay, no need to be sorry. I told you, didn't I? I didn't mind that little scratch."

"If you say so... My orders are to keep an eye on the Dragon Princess. Nothing about you. Personally, I don't want to hurt you. You don't have to worry about me attacking you at school. I'm not going to start anything with her, either, while we're here. You can trust me."

"Ah..."

Ryuunosuke looked up sideways at the ceiling, feeling bad about his frightened reaction to her. He scratched the back of his head.

"I've always trusted you, from the moment we met. I just...wasn't expecting to see you, that's all."

"That's a relief to hear..."

For a few moments, sweet silence fell between them.

"On a different topic...would you like to go out for ramen with me at Saburou's one of these days—?"

But she didn't get to finish.

"You there."

They hadn't noticed Rinne walking up to them. She was giving Mari a death stare. She grabbed one of Ryuunosuke's arms, and Mari clutched his other one. He was sandwiched between the two girls.

"Get away from Ryuunosuke, impudent wench."

Mari frowned angrily.

"And why do you think you have the right to order me around? What I do with Ryuunosuke Dazai is none of your business, so shut it, lizard."

"You talk big for a frail little bat who lost to me and ran away squealing."

"Excuse me? Oh, don't tell me you thought I was fighting you for real back then? I couldn't use my full strength with Ryuunosuke Dazai there. Wasn't that obvious? I guess your reptile brain is too tiny to understand that."

"I do not know what sort of relationship you *think* you have with Ryuunosuke..."

"...Yeah, go on?"

"...but he is destined to be my mate. He has wed me."

"What?! He MARRIED you?!"

Mari quickly turned to look at Ryuunosuke. Her eyes were open wide in shock. He raised his hands placatingly.

"Calm down, Abara. It's not what she meant."

"R-right, I didn't believe it for a moment that you'd marry this primitive animal. You belong to me after all," Mari said, still seeming shaken.

"He has wed me, not you."

"He probably just said whatever to get you off him!"

"I have also heard you are a first-year student. I am a second-year student. You should treat me with respect, as I am your senior."

"Shut up, idiot! I'd rather die than be polite to you!"

It looked like they were about to start throwing punches, but what

worried Ryuunosuke more than that was the fact that other students around were getting curious why one of the girls was claiming to be married to him. He wanted to shout, "It's not what it sounds like! It's just soul linking! Not marriage!" But he couldn't do that, of course.

"Heh… You must be very envious of my relationship with Ryuunosuke. Do not chew off all your fingernails watching us enjoy our honeymoon."

"Grrr! Ryuunosuke Dazai! You're not opposed to polygamy, are you?!"

"Calm down, Abara! If anything, it'd be, um…poly-soul-y?"

The girls glared at each other, standing so close that their breasts were touching. Mari's gaze dropped down to Rinne's chest.

"Hmm, not much there, huh?"

"Hmm? What do you mean?"

Frustration changed to gloating in Mari's eyes as she pointedly stared at Rinne's breasts with a faint smile on her lips.

"What…? Shameless wench! Thinking herself superior just because her chest is a little bigger…!"

"Don't feel bad—you just can't help it, being a reptile."

"I am not an animal; I am a dragon. You are also mistaken in assuming Ryuunosuke would be swayed by some superfluous blubber!"

"Wrong, sweetie. Based on the images saved on Ryuunosuke's phone, blond hair and big busts are what he likes best. Sorry, but I win in this department."

"R-Ryuunosuke! Explain!"

"Abara, you have some explaining to do, too! How do you know what's on my phone?"

"It's your own fault for setting your birthday as your PIN."

Almost reduced to tears, Ryuunosuke made a mental note to change his PIN as soon as possible.

"His… His preference will surely change under the effect of my love…"

"Oh yeah? Come on, just admit defeat and move on. Don't turn into mush from your salty tears, like a slug."

"If I am a slug, you are a mosquito. Or no, a chupacabra."

"A what? I bet it's something nasty, isn't it...?"

Somehow, Ryuunosuke found their bickering calming, never mind the content. At a glance, there was no way these girls would get along—they seemed to hate each other's guts. But compared with their almost deadly battle, taunting each other in the school hallway was kind of cute. Ryuunosuke felt so comforted, he thought that having two equally pretty girls verbally tearing each other apart right next to him was uniquely nourishing for his soul.

"Sputter angrily as much as you want—your words cannot damage my confidence."

"And why do you feel so confident, huh?"

"Heh. I am glad you asked."

Rinne brushed back her hair and looked at Mari haughtily.

"I will tell you."

"It's going to be something stupid nobody cares about, I bet."

Mari crossed her arms, staring at Rinne with distaste.

"Ryuunosuke and I are living together. He has even seen me naked."

Rinne smiled victoriously.

"WHAT...?!"

Mari gasped at this critical attack.

"Don't make it sound weird! We're just sharing rooms, and we've had a little incident, that's all!" Ryuunosuke said desperately.

The classroom erupted in an uproar.

"No way... She only just arrived, and my crush has already been stolen..."

"And he's not even, like, good at humanities, despite that fancy name..."

"Aren't you going to fight back, Aya? Are you going to let that girl take Ryuunosuke from you?!"

"Wh-what are you talking about?!"

"Dazai, you and I are buddies no matter what!"

Ryuunosuke pretended not to hear all those comments. The person most upset about him living with Rinne was the blond vampire, though.

"Wh-wh-wh-what?! Ryuunosuke Dazai! Why did you give yourself to another woman when you already have me?!"

"Don't talk like we're together, Abara! Come on, you have a good head on your shoulders; surely, you can piece together why she ended up in my house!"

"I'm sorry, you're right. Emotions clouded my judgment. I get it; it makes sense that she's living with you. I'd have arranged it that way, too, if I wasn't in the other camp."

"But I have not told you everything yet," Rinne interrupted.

"There's more?!"

Rinne nodded. Her cheeks flushed red, and she began to twiddle her fingers.

"This morning," she began quietly, "Ryuunosuke touched my...special places."

"He did WHAT?!"

She meant the dragon body parts, but it sounded very sketchy. Ryuunosuke had no way of undoing the damage her statement brought.

"Rinne, you shouldn't be telling everyone!"

"Ryuunosuke Dazai! Touch me, too!"

"Don't be ridiculous, Abara!"

Between Rinne, who was innocently saying the most outrageous things, and Mari, who was starting to act totally deranged, Ryuunosuke couldn't keep up. His classmates were staring at him with either curiosity or hatred. He pretended not to notice.

"I hated to see him even talk to other girls... Can't describe what I'm feeling now..."

"What do I need to do to have girls fighting over me...?"

"Aya, is this true?!"

"I... I saw her sitting on top of him this morning. She was half naked..."

"Sorry, Dazai, but I'm seriously going to kill you."

Ryuunosuke heard his childhood friend Aya sell him out, but that didn't make much of a difference. His reputation in class was already scraping rock-bottom, and almost everyone was looking at him with disgust.

"It is settled, then. I win," said Rinne.

"No, you don't! I won't accept defeat, ever!"

"What's this commotion? Get back to your seats, everyone," the English teacher said, walking into the room.

Ryuunosuke had been saved—for now.

◆

The third period was physical education. At West Kokonoe High, different years had physical education classes together a few times each year to encourage older and younger students to get to know each other. That day, first-year and second-year students had their class together. Gym uniforms were different colors depending on the years—first-years wore red, second-years blue, and third-years green.

The sports grounds had been divided into two halves, one for boys to practice high jump, and the other for girls to do shot put.

Ryuunosuke was sitting in a corner, waiting his turn and idly watching the girls—or rather, it'd be more precise to say he was watching Rinne and Mari. It was Rinne's turn to throw. He wanted to see how that would go.

The girl's physical education class was progressing smoothly. The shot-put area was marked with chalk lines and a circle where the thrower would stand. A girl in a sports jersey lifted the shot to her chin level. She stepped back, turned her body so that she was facing away from the direction she'd be throwing the ball, and then spun around and threw it. The ball traced an arc in the air and then fell to the ground. Two girls tasked with measuring the distance ran toward the ball with a long measuring tape, and another girl went to retrieve the ball.

"Irako, you're next."

"Yes, ma'am."

Irako, who had been sitting with her knees drawn up to her chin, stood when the teacher called her name.

"I will get ready."

"Good luck!" Aya, who'd been next to her, cheered her on.

When Ryuunosuke wasn't around, Aya kept Rinne company, helping her get used to the new surroundings. Aya gave Rinne lots of attention—maybe because she felt responsible for her as the first girl from the school whom Rinne had met, or because she liked to help others, or both—and the two girls quickly became friends.

In contrast with Aya, there was one student who did everything she could to keep her distance from Rinne.

"Let's see if the fire-breathing lizard can do it…"

It was Mari, of course. Surrounded by girls from her year, she was observing Rinne. She was frowning, but from worry rather than hostility.

"Hope she doesn't stir up trouble…"

Oblivious to Mari's intense stare, Rinne walked to the middle of the circle on the ground and casually picked up the four-kilogram shot for girl's shot put. She swung her arm far back in preparation for the throw when someone interrupted her.

"N-no, stop, you idiot dragon princess!" Mari shouted in a panicked voice, running up to her.

Rinne looked at her questioningly.

"What do you want? Hmm… That jersey looks atrocious on you."

"Don't make me punch you in the face! What were you planning to do with the ball? Just throw it like this?"

"It is a contest where one throws this iron ball and the distance is measured, correct? I may not have experience, but I can do it just as well as anyone."

Rinne puffed her chest out, feeling confident.

"Didn't you notice how the others were throwing it?"

"I have been watching. The other girls threw the ball in a way that compensates for their lack of strength."

"At least you got that."

"But I do not need to replicate their way of throwing to get the ball past that fence over there. The farthest any girl has thrown the ball so far was about eight meters. If I throw it past the fence, I should be able to set an unbeatable record. As far as I can tell, only you may be able to rival me."

"Thanks for the super-long analysis, it made it perfectly clear that you're a total idiot. Give me that for a moment."

"What...?"

Mari snatched the shot from her. She looked at it closely and groaned. Rinne's fingers had left indents in the iron ball.

"What high school girl can poke holes in the shot with her fingers?!"

"I can?"

"You really make me want to whack your stupid head!"

"What are you doing there, Abara?" the PE teacher called suspiciously.

"I'm just showing this idio— I'm just showing the new girl how to do this! I'll be right back! Ha-ha... Ha-ha-ha!"

Mari's fake laugh quickly died, and she looked into Rinne's eyes with dead seriousness.

"Listen," she said. "While we're here, we have to pretend we're ordinary girls."

"Ordinary...?"

"That's right. If you can't do that, you can't live out here in the big world. And normal girls can't do an overhand shot throw or make marks in the iron ball with their fingers!"

"I suppose I have not adjusted to 'normal.'"

"Duh."

Mari could only guess whether Rinne meant she was capable of adjusting her behavior to pass as normal, or if she was a hopeless case. It was clear to Mari, though, that this time, it was down to her to do something.

"Oh, bother... All right." She sighed.

Her thought process was as follows.

Why do I have to babysit her? But if I just ignore her, she'll cause trouble

*for both of us. I'd better make sure she doesn't. It really shouldn't be my job,
but I guess I'll do it this time.*

"Let me show you how to do it correctly. Miss! The new girl hasn't
done this before. Is it okay if I throw first to demonstrate?"

The teacher gave her the go-ahead, and Mari entered the circle.

"Here goes!" she shouted in a sweet voice and threw the shot with
perfect form.

Had she used her full strength, she could've easily thrown the shot
past the school fence. This time, though, it landed not far off from where
the other students had thrown it.

Rinne covered her mouth to conceal a smug smile.

"Heh. Pathetic."

"You're really asking for it, grrr!"

"Bwuh, pfweh!"

Rinne made unintelligible noises as Mari grabbed her by the cheeks,
pulling and squishing her face.

Ryuunosuke, who'd been watching the girls' interaction from his
side of the sports grounds, nodded to himself.

"No idea what they were talking about, but seeing them like this,
they're just like any other girls…"

He rubbed the bridge of his nose, thinking about how Mari and
Rinne seemed to be getting along, even though just the other night,
they had been trying to kill each other. He nodded to himself again
and touched his left ring finger, where the light ring had been. It had
disappeared, but he still felt that "something" was there on his finger.
Thanks to the power of the ring, Rinne could enjoy school life. If he
could use this power to help other mythical girls lead ordinary lives, he'd
be happy to do that.

It was his turn to jump. He ran up to the bar and cleared it beau-
tifully with the Fosbury flop. When he was upside down, he caught a
glimpse of Rinne and Mari arguing over something.

"Like two old friends!"

◆

After fourth period, they had lunchtime. Ryuunosuke brought Rinne to the school canteen. It and the main building had been remodeled and now looked like a cross between a stylish café and a restaurant. Their clientele was made up of chatty, high-energy teens with big appetites, though, so it didn't have the sort of refined, relaxing atmosphere you'd expect based on the interior design.

Ryuunosuke and Rinne joined the line for the meal-ticket machine. Rinne was uneasy, maybe because she wasn't used to being in busy places like that. She was holding tight to Ryuunosuke's sleeve. The line was moving slowly, but they eventually made it to the machine.

"What do you want to eat, Rinne? It's your first day of school, so I'll treat you! Um, I don't actually know what's on the menu today, though."

"I do not know, either… I would like the same meal you will be having."

"Okay! I can tell you that the best value for money here is the meat-feast set. Girls don't seem to go for that one much, though."

They took the tickets to the counter, joining another line until the staff handed them trays with chopsticks and the meat feasts.

"Great, let's eat! Um, but wait…" Ryuunosuke tried to spot a free table. "It's really full. Wish I'd thought of finding a table first."

The canteen was busier than usual that day, and all tables were already taken. Ryuunosuke had always managed to find a table even at the busiest of times in the past, so he'd gone to get food first before checking.

"Ryuunosuke, how about there?"

Rinne pointed to the corner, where there was a free table for four. They carried their trays there, but someone set their tray on it the same time they did.

"Yikes. It's the lousy lunkhead lizard…"

"The blond blockhead bat…"

*   *   *

Mari Abara was like their shadow that day. The two pretty girls sat down next to each other, cringing. Ryuunosuke chose the seat opposite Rinne, already expecting trouble.

Mari had a bowl of ramen on her tray, with all the toppings available at their school—doubled.

"Hey, why don't you go sit somewhere else?" Mari whined.

"Why should I? I sat down here first," Rinne argued.

"I found this table first! But all right, I'll put up with sharing the table with you if Ryuunosuke Dazai moves to sit opposite me."

"Huh? Sure, I can move." Ryuunosuke stood up, but Rinne stopped him.

"He is staying where he is."

"What do you care?!"

While the girls argued, Ryuunosuke became conscious of the people watching them. They were curious about the boy sitting with the two beauties, and then they recognized him as the student council vice president.

"Let me tell you something, Ryuunosuke Dazai," Mari said to him suddenly.

"What is it?"

"Mythical girls always fight, no matter who they are. I know other mythical girls, and we're also always fighting."

Rinne looked at Mari with wide eyes.

"Really?"

"Why don't you know that? Never mind. There are exceptions, I guess."

Ryuunosuke really wished Mari and Rinne could be friends, but then again, Rinne was allied with the Calamity Research Institute, and Mari with the Order, which made friendship difficult, unfortunately. He wondered if them acting like friends during the physical education class was a one-off and they were destined to be enemies forever. His palms became sweaty.

"Maybe we won't be able to get along like one happy family after all..."

"Why are you muttering to yourself, Ryuunosuke Dazai?"

"Thank you for this meal," Rinne said, pressing her palms together.

Ryuunosuke was about to start eating without saying anything, but he stopped and put his chopsticks down.

"You know the proper etiquette...," he said with surprise.

"What do you mean?"

Rinne was about to eat a piece of fried chicken, but she stopped, holding it with her chopsticks in the air.

"You said 'thank you' before eating."

"It is the polite thing to say, is it not? Expressing gratitude for food. Ranko taught me this."

Ryuunosuke reflected on how he'd grown up without learning proper manners, and he felt bad.

"Enjoy your food, everyone," he said after a pause, picking up his chopsticks again.

The canteen meat feast he and Rinne were eating consisted of deep-fried chicken, grilled beef, stir-fried pork with ginger sauce, a big helping of shredded cabbage, and rice.

Rinne held up one of the two big chunks of fried chicken and took a bite.

"Mmm!"

"You like it?"

"It is so delicious!" she replied with stars in her eyes.

"Yesss! Rinne, that reaction gets a ten out of ten! A beautiful girl exposed to junk food for the first time melts in delight—exactly what I wanted to see! Really glad you went for the meat feast. I'll enjoy my food twice as much just picturing your delicious reaction in my head!"

"Sometimes, you say really weird stuff, Ryuunosuke Dazai...," Mari said. Then she noticed Rinne staring intently at her ramen. "Huh? What... What do you want?"

"Some of your ramen."

"Seriously? Ugh, okay, in exchange for a piece of fried chicken."

"Here."

Rinne held up the half-eaten piece of chicken with her chopsticks, bringing it to Mari's mouth.

"Hey, I don't want the one you already took a bite out of! Eh, whatever." She chomped down on it. "Oh, it is pretty good. Maybe I'll go for the meat feast next time."

"See, it is good food. Now you give me your ramen."

"Okay, okay. But only one spoonful!"

She scooped up some noodles and toppings with her spoon and brought it to Rinne's mouth.

"Mmm! This is also very tasty!"

"Of course it is."

"But the amount you gave me was unfairly small. Give me that slice of egg, too."

"What?! Want to fight?!"

"Anytime."

"Hold on. You've got a bit of spring onion on your face. Turn this way."

"Okay."

Mari took out her hankie and wiped the onion off the corner of Rinne's mouth. Ryuunosuke watched them, his palms no longer sweaty.

"You two… Do you like each other after all…?"

Any bystander would think it cute how these two pretty girls shared their food. They would never imagine the girls ever attempting to kill each other. When Ryuunosuke asked that question, though, they stopped smiling and shook their heads. Simultaneously.

"A preposterous suggestion, Ryuunosuke."

"Yeah, what were you thinking, Ryuunosuke Dazai? We might look like friends, but seriously, I could never be friends with someone like her."

"I fully agree. There can never be friendship between me and a leech like you."

"Or between me and a scaly worm like you."

"Well, looks like we have something in common after all…!"

"Oh, suuure…!"

The girls pinched each other's cheeks, glaring daggers even as they forced their lips into a smile.

"Ryuunosuke Dazai! Would you like me to feed you some of my ramen, too?"

"What?! No, I want to feed him!"

"Er, thanks, but I'm okay. Watching you feed each other was satisfying enough."

"Are you not hungry anymore, Ryuunosuke? Can I have the rest of your food, then?"

"No, I'm still eating this. You sound like President; she was after my chicken one time last year, too…"

He promptly stuffed the last bit of his fried chicken into his mouth, thinking that despite what they said, Rinne and Mari did like each other.

"President, huh… That reminds me, I wanted to ask you something," Mari began.

"You do not need to answer any of the chupacabra's questions, Ryuunosuke," Rinne interrupted.

"Stop butting in! I looked up what a chupacabra is, by the way. Gross! Nothing like a vampire."

"If it is gross, then it is exactly like a vampire."

"Shut up!"

"So, Abara? What did you want to ask me about?" asked Ryuunosuke, to get back on topic.

"Ah, right. So Ranko told you about last night?"

"No? What about last night? Something to do with Rinne?"

Mari froze for a moment.

"Um… Y-yeah. Never mind."

She stood up, picking up her tray.

"I'm finished eating. Not going to stick around, because although I like you, Ryuunosuke Dazai, I'm not her friend."

She turned away from them and went to return her tray. She thanked the school cook for the meal and left the canteen.

"I wonder why she left so suddenly."

"Who knows? Perhaps she was deeply hurt by me calling her a chupacabra."

"I don't think so… If she didn't mind you almost killing her last night, I don't think calling her silly names would hurt her. Besides, it's not like *chupacabra* is even offensive..."

◆

The classes ended, and Ryuunosuke and Rinne headed to the student council room. Ryuunosuke had work he needed to finish that day. Aya was going to stop by her club room before joining them.

"Ranko has explained the student council's function, and I have also read about it. It is a group of students with authority over all the other students in their school...," Rinne said with admiration.

"Maybe in anime, but not in real life..." At first, Ryuunosuke wanted to correct her skewed image of the student council, but when he thought twice about it, he changed tack. "No, wait, you are absolutely right. We rule the school. Nobody can tell us what to do."

"Of course not, with Ranko as your boss..."

Rinne swallowed audibly.

The truth was, the student council had no authority over anyone, and their tasks included organizing school events, drafting the budget for them, and looking after school equipment. Ryuunosuke had lied just to see Rinne's reaction. It wasn't as if she was going to join the council, so it wasn't important for her to have accurate information on what the council could or could not do.

They opened the door to the student council room. Everything inside looked the same as usual. Someone was already there.

"There you are, Dazai boy, Rinne."

It was Ranko, who had said she'd be staying at Ryuunosuke's home that day. She was sitting in her usual chair, doing some paperwork.

"Thought you weren't coming today."

"I got here not that long ago. It's good that you've both come here together."

"Oh?"

"I was going to call for Rinne. You saved me the trouble, bringing her here. Please take a seat."

Ryuunosuke picked up a folded chair from the corner and carried it to the table for Rinne. They both sat down.

"You wished to see me, Ranko?"

"That's right. Tell me, how was your first day at school?"

"I encountered no issues. It was a success."

"…"

Ryuunosuke internally disagreed with that, but he didn't say anything. Ranko noticed the look in his eyes, and a little smile appeared on her lips.

"Heh. That's good to hear, Rinne."

"But why did you want to call here to the student council room, President?"

"To have her join the council, naturally."

"Rinne is joining the student council?"

"Yes. I've already registered her."

"Well, that was quick…"

"I have been granted…the student council powers?!"

Rinne's eyes shone with excitement, while Ryuunosuke was still trying to wrap his head around this sudden appointment.

"She will be acting as—"

Ranko was interrupted by the door opening. Two girls entered the room.

"Hel-lo there! Here comes the world-class beauty… Wait, ugh. I forgot about this idiot. What's she doing here…?"

"Good morning! Hello, Rinne."

It was Mari and Aya. Ranko smiled and waved at Mari, who just made a face in response.

"Weren't you going to your club, Isurugi?" Ranko asked.

"I was, but then I ran into Mari. I don't have much to do at the club today anyway, so I thought I'd come here with Mari first and meet my club friends later."

"So it's not just me who gets bossed around by Abara…," Ryuunosuke mused.

"She should be here for our meeting instead of wandering off to some club! It was lucky I caught her," Mari said in her defense.

"It's okay, I don't mind, if it makes Mari happy."

They sat down at the table, with Aya opposite Ryuunosuke and Mari next to him. He now had Rinne on one side, and Mari on the other.

"Ranko, you were going to announce my role. I have been told that you are the president of the council, Ryuunosuke is the vice president, and Aya is the secretary...," Rinne trailed off.

"Hold up! Why is this moron making it sound like she's going to be on the council?!"

"M-Mari! You're being very rude! She's your senior, too...," Aya scolded.

Mari grabbed Ryuunosuke's arm and was looking past him at Rinne threateningly.

"Don't try to dispute it, Mari, it's already decided. And anyhow, you're in no position to question my decisions," Ranko said bluntly.

"Grrr..."

Mari quieted down after Ranko told her off.

"Rinne's job will be..."

Ranko paused for effect.

"...vice president's assistant."

For a moment, there was complete silence.

"She can't be that!!!" Mari yelled. "That's my job! Ryuunosuke Dazai needs only one assistant, and that's me! I'm not sharing with her!"

Mari was gesticulating wildly, like a child having a tantrum.

"I also find it disagreeable to share this position with her," Rinne chimed in with her own opinion.

"You can't be his assistant! Only I can!"

"Ridiculous. Ryuunosuke and I are bound by our vows to support each other throughout our lives. Therefore, I am the most qualified to help him in his job as a student council vice president."

"Screw you!"

"I'll be outnumbered by my assistants...," Ryuunosuke complained as Mari and Rinne fought.

Aya snorted a laugh, no longer able to keep pretending she wasn't listening.

"Since I have been given this position, I shall carry out my duties with care and commitment. I shall prove to that vampire I am better suited to assist Ryuunosuke both in battle and in his student council role."

"Oh yeah? I've been his assistant all this time until you showed up, you clueless, sorry excuse for a dragon!"

Aya cocked her head.

"Ryuu," she asked. "Why are they calling each other a vampire and a dragon?"

"Er... Who knows what's going on in their heads? Ha-ha..."

When the arguing stopped, Ranko and Aya busied themselves with the paperwork. For some reason, Rinne and Mari moved their chairs closer to Ryuunosuke, so that their shoulders were pressing against his.

"Sorry, but it's kind of hard for me to work like this...," he protested thinly, feeling cramped.

"Please carry on with your work. I will support you," Rinne said reassuringly.

"I will support you better than her," Mari insisted.

"Right, but... You see, I don't need you physically supporting me in my chair, you know?"

"You are sweating, Ryuunosuke. Let me wipe your face."

"I'm sweating because you're crowding me in..."

He did nothing to resist Rinne wiping sweat off his brow.

"Are you thirsty, Ryuunosuke Dazai? Have some of my drink."

"No, I'm oka— Mngh!"

Mari forcefully wedged the straw of her sports drink into his mouth.

"I feel like a patient being tended to by two overly eager hospital nurses!"

"Your words are too kind, Ryuunosuke. You are making me blush..."

"You made me smile, too, Ryuunosuke Dazai..."

"I didn't mean it as praise!"

◆

The hellish student council duties eventually ended, and Ryuunosuke left with Rinne.

"What do you want for dinner, Rinne?"

"Will you be making it for us?"

"I guess so… Something's telling me President won't volunteer to cook. She doesn't seem the type. Or do you want to cook?"

"Ha-ha-ha-ha! Ryuunosuke, you joker. I cannot cook, obviously."

"Figures…"

"I will be happy with anything you cook."

"Anything, huh…? Listen, Rinne. Telling the person who's going to do the cooking that anything is fine is the most unhelpful. What sort of food did you have at the research facility?"

"I was served dishes like spinach salad with sesame dressing, julienned daikon stew, and boiled mustard greens."

"That's what you get for hospital meals, right? By the way, do you have to check in at the hospital—no, I mean, the research facility first?"

"Yes. We both have to undergo regular checkups."

Rinne would be having medical examinations to see whether she was progressing toward berserk status, while Ryuunosuke would be a test subject for the research on Sacred Sealing Rings. It was only because he readily agreed to this that Ryuunosuke was allowed to go free.

"The train station is the pickup point… I wish President was coming with us, but she left early in a hurry."

"She must be extremely busy with work beyond our imagination."

"Yeah, I bet. We have some time to kill. Let's do grocery shopping on the way home after the checkups."

"That sounds like a good plan."

Ryuunosuke heard a message notification. He checked his phone and saw a text from Ranko.

"Huh? Ranko wrote, *'I sent you money for helping with my research. Check your bank account. Make sure to keep receipts of all expenses.'* Wow, cool."

Ranko had told him before that he'd be compensated for his help, and since he was broke, Ryuunosuke welcomed any extra income. He was helping because he thought it was the right thing to do, but he wouldn't turn down a cash incentive.

Ryuunosuke and Rinne headed to the West Kokonoe train station. There were the usual stores you'd expect near a station, like a general store, supermarket, fast-food restaurants, and a bookstore. Ryuunosuke went to check his account balance at a bank ATM. A little excited, he waited for the display to show him how much money he got from Ranko.

"What...?"

He rubbed his eyes and checked the numbers again. After that, he printed a statement and took it from the machine with shaking hands, checking the numbers one more time.

"Is something the matter?"

"Uh... Let's get out of here, Rinne..."

He took Rinne by the hand and left the bank, looking around suspiciously. He dragged Rinne with him until he found a quiet back alley with no one else around.

"Why did you lead me to this dark alley...? Oh! Ryuunosuke... You want to do it here...?!"

"No! I don't want to do THAT sort of stuff! Wait a minute, okay?"

He took out the printed account statement, slowly unfolded it, and examined it carefully.

"I'm not dreaming..."

The amount Ranko had wired him was way higher than what he'd been expecting. It was so much, he began to wonder if he'd have to pay tax on it.

"Pay's good in our line of work."

Ryuunosuke jumped when someone suddenly spoke to him.
"Eep!"

Pathetically, he hid behind Rinne's back. From there, he finally dared to look at the person who had approached them.

"Hey, it's just Mr. Sarashina... Don't sneak up on us like that—you scared the daylights out of me! Hello, by the way."

"Hi."

It was Suberu Sarashina, a medical researcher from the Calamity Research Institute. Rinne bowed to him.

"I wasn't expecting to see you here," Ryuunosuke said.

"I came to pick you up, thinking you'd prefer someone you've already met. Next time, someone else from the department will come to get you. We'd be early if we went now. Are you ready, or should I get you a bit later?"

"We don't have anything else to do right now, so we can just go. Is that okay with you, Rinne?"

"Yes, I am ready to go."

Suberu led them to a nearby parking lot, where they got into a large black car. Suberu was driving, and Rinne and Ryuunosuke sat in the back. The car was so spacious, they could stretch out their legs easily. They could see a familiar nightscape out the windows. Ryuunosuke wondered if it was Suberu's own car or if it belonged to the Calamity Research Institute. He couldn't tell.

"What sort of job do you do, Mr. Sarashina?" Ryuunosuke asked just to make conversation.

"My job is to save the world!" Suberu boomed back proudly, his voice sounding louder on account of being in such a small, enclosed space.

Ryuunosuke was a bit surprised by that grandiose statement.

"Right, mythical girls are a threat to the world. Your job's pretty cool! And President—I mean, Ranko is only a little older than me, but she's working on that research with you. Isn't she amazing, Rinne?"

"Yes. She is, without doubt, an incredible person."

"A genius, even. By the way, Ryuunosuke. You're also going to have a checkup today? How are you feeling? Anything worrying you?" Suberu asked.

"Um... It's just my ring that's going to be examined, not myself."

"What ring?"

"Huh? Ranko didn't tell you?"

"She didn't tell me anything about any rings," Suberu replied, confused.

Rinne frowned, incredulous.

"Oh, well, maybe it's unimportant...," Ryuunosuke said to him. *That's really weird*, he thought. *They're coworkers, but Mr. Sarashina doesn't know about the Sacred Sealing Rings...*

They sat in silence as Suberu drove along the highway.

◆

Later that evening, Ryuunosuke, Rinne, and Ranko headed back home together after Ranko carried out the checkups on them.

The examinations turned out to be more thorough and down-to-earth than Ryuunosuke had been expecting. He was put into a machine that looked like an MRI scanner, made to drink a bitter medicine, and scanned in another machine where he had to turn around, like for a barium X-ray.

On the way home, they bought groceries for dinner, which didn't go smoothly at all, but that's another story. After dinner, Ryuunosuke washed the dishes while Ranko and Rinne stayed at the low dining table, enjoying some tea.

"You're a good cook, Dazai boy."

"I second that. The meal was delicious."

Both girls had eaten their fill. Ryuunosuke had made deep-fried chicken with sweet-and-sour sauce, fried eggs with tomato over rice, and a pea-sprout-and-fried-tofu salad.

"Heh-heh! I've learned a few tricks working part-time in a restaurant," he said nonchalantly, but the truth was, he was super happy that they liked the food.

It had been quite a while since Ryuunosuke last cooked at home. For a long time, he'd had to drastically save on food, since he had no money, but he really did enjoy cooking. Because he could now get reimbursed for groceries, he'd gone all out on the meal for the three of them.

"Hurry up with the dishes, Ryuunosuke, and give me some attention."

"He'll finish quicker if you help him, Rinne."

"Oh…! Dividing the task between more people will make it quicker, of course! I am in awe of your intellect, Ranko."

Rinne swiftly got to her feet and went over to help Ryuunosuke.

"Be thankful, Ryuunosuke! I am going to assist you!"

"I like your enthusiasm, I guess! Thanks."

"I shall do my utmost. Watch and marvel!"

Rinne picked up a dirty plate from the sink.

"Aah?!"

This was the girl who had thrown a cargo container and left marks in an iron ball with her fingers. The plate couldn't withstand her dragon power. It shattered into countless pieces.

"R-Ryuunosukeee…"

"Looks like you were a bit too energetic this time… How come the dishes at the canteen survived you, I wonder…?"

"Uh… I am filled with shame…"

"Hey, don't worry about it. I'll wash and wipe the dishes, and you put them in the cupboard. How about that?"

"Understood… I will put the dishes away."

Rinne dejectedly walked back to the dining table, where Ranko was doing something on her phone.

"President, I forgot to tell you I don't have broadband. You probably need to be online for your work, right? Are you going to be okay just using your phone data?" Ryuunosuke asked.

"No need. Here, this is our Wi-Fi password."

She placed a piece of paper on the table.

"What do you mean 'our' Wi-Fi? Do I not know about something?"

"I got broadband for your crummy house."

"What?!"

"I also had AC installed in my room and in the living room."

"Whaaat?!"

Ryuunosuke looked around the living room in surprise.

"Oh, there it is! How did I miss it? I guess I conditioned myself not to pay too much attention to my house! It's right next to the clock! A modern convenience like that in my own home! By the way, you meant MY room, right?!"

"Don't worry about the cost. That goes with the expenses."

"I didn't ask for any of that, but thank you. You do remember this is still MY house, right?!"

"Getting the broadband and AC units installed in just one day was a piece of cake compared with enrolling Rinne as a student despite her not having any public school records."

"I didn't ask you if it was easy or not! This is rented accommodation, you know! I hope the landlords don't get mad..."

"If you get any complaints, I'll handle them."

Ryuunosuke wanted to avoid getting her involved in any landlord disputes. He had a feeling it would escalate out of proportion.

Ranko stood. She put on a jacket and picked up her bag.

"Well, I'll be going now."

"What? Where? We just got back."

"Rinne broke one of your plates. I'm going out to buy a replacement."

"You absolutely hate tedious errands, and yet you want to go out late at night to buy me a new plate? I appreciate that, but why don't you go tomorrow?"

"Oh dear. Dazai boy, you are so clueless. Learn to have a little more sensitivity, or you won't win any hearts."

"He does not need to win any hearts. He already has mine, and that is enough," Rinne cut in.

"Heh. Yes, of course. Buying a new plate is just an excuse. I need to obtain some necessary commodities for myself. Girls need all sorts of things boys don't for their daily life."

"Okay, got it. Wait, but you don't have a key," Ryuunosuke noted.

"I got a set of keys cut for me already."

She took a key ring from her pocket to show him. It had a poop mascot character attached.

"Right. I should've guessed."

"Be careful outside, Ranko. It may be dangerous at night."

"Thank you, Rinne. It's kind of you to worry about me. I'll be careful."

"I—I did not speak out of kindness. Merely out of concern, because I would not wish to lose my caretaker."

"Sure, let's leave it at that. I'll try to be back as soon as I can, sweetie. Dazai boy, stay out of my room. It's a mess."

"It's MY room!"

Ranko waved and went out.

Ryuunosuke was done with the dishes. He wiped his hands on his apron and sat down opposite Rinne, taking out his smartphone. He talked to her while tapping on it.

"Wow, we really have Wi-Fi... The SSID is *ChunkyPoop*... Makes me not want to connect to it. President has the sense of humor of a five-year-old..."

"I do not know what this 'why fie' is... Did Ranko do something to upset you?"

"No, I'm really glad she got my house online. I've been having to watch my data usage—couldn't really use the internet much on my phone before. I haven't even touched it since yesterday. But I really wish President asked me before making changes to my house."

"I think you are aware of this, but you have Ranko to thank for letting you return to your house. If it was not for her, you might have been put in a solitary room in the basement of the Calamity Research Institute's facility, as a study subject. The organization is interested in obtaining data about soul linkers and Sacred Sealing Rings, not in your well-being."

"Linkers are legendary-level rare, right? President said so when she was examining me."

"Which is why the council...the Calamity Research Institute's bosses were opposed to letting you go free with me after I reached berserk phase one, but Ranko quickly managed to convince them and get approval for the Dragon Babysitter Project."

Rinne seemed very proud of Ranko.

"You two have this sisterly vibe. Ranko looks like she should be your younger sister, though."

"Do you think so? Hmm. Perhaps. She is the only person I would consider a true friend. She was the first friend I made at the facility."

"Really?"

"When she was assigned to the Calamity Research Institute, she came to see me and, despite the other researchers trying to stop her, shook my hand. She said to me then, *I'd like to be your friend.*' It was preposterous for a researcher to enter the cell where a dangerous creature such as myself was being kept. She is very intelligent, but sometimes, she commits such acts of folly. Well, we did become friends then." Rinne shared her treasured memories with Ryuunosuke, wistfulness in her tone.

"She was probably the only one who never saw you as a dangerous monster."

"...Yes. You are right."

Rinne lowered her eyelids, and she smiled.

"President really is something else. She approached me on my first day at school, saying she liked me and wanted me on the student council. She instantly closes the distance with you, know what I mean? Right off the bat, we had a great vibe going. She's like this with everyone."

"I do not enjoy you speaking with admiration about other females, even Ranko. Apologize, Ryuunosuke."

"What?! But we were both talking about how cool she is!"

Ryuunosuke was so taken aback by Rinne's abrupt demand that he recoiled, lifting both his hands, and fell backward onto the floor. Rinne considered him for a moment. Then she got up and walked over to where he was on the floor. She sat down on him, bending to look at his face.

"Ryuunosuke."

"Wh-what is it?"

Rinne's long hair was tickling his face. She was staring into his eyes with a fiery intensity.

"This will be our first night together...since we have paired up."

"Right. I'll leave you here; you can have this room to yourself."

Ryuunosuke got a bad feeling and tried to escape.

"Wait."

She stopped him, grabbing his arm.

"Ranko has seen to our sleeping arrangements. She prepared two futons...but we need only one, do we not?"

"Ow, ow, ow, ow! Why do you have to be...so much stronger than me?! I just want to have a bath. Let me go and have a bath!"

"Ah. I understand."

"Er... Do you, really?!"

She let him go. Ryuunosuke left his phone on the dining table and escaped to the changing room.

◆

Rinne was left alone in the living room. The earlier ruckus was just a memory, replaced by silence.

"The silence that follows accentuates the welcome liveliness of being together with friends..."

Rinne was keenly aware of how lucky she was to be able to enjoy a normal life after the progression of her berserk phase and ultimate confinement. She was shyly allowing herself to imagine a future where she was allowed to live, where her being alive would not lead to the destruction of the world.

"Hmm...?"

Her gaze fell on Ryuunosuke's smartphone, which he had left behind on the table. The home screen was bright—Ryuunosuke had forgotten to lock the phone.

Rinne picked it up.

"It looks very different from the model I was given..."

Ryuunosuke's phone was a very old model from a cheap brand.

Rinne's phone was a different version and had a different interface and features.

Rinne suddenly remembered what Mari had said before, at school.

Based on the images saved on Ryuunosuke's phone...

Rinne gulped, looking at the phone in her hand.

"Maybe I could take a little peek..."

She felt the urge to check if Mari was telling the truth about Ryuunosuke's taste in women.

"No, no. Perish the thought. That would be a disrespectful violation of privacy... I must not lower myself to the level of that shameless bloodsucker."

Rinne shook her head and put the phone back down on the table. Her fingertips accidentally brushed against the screen, opening the browser. It displayed the page Ryuunosuke had viewed the night before—the comments under a news article about a killer being sentenced to death. Rinne couldn't help reading one of the comments.

```
Some people don't deserve to live.
```

◆

A girl was sitting at a table for two at Chandelier, a diner outside the West Kokonoe train station. She looked decidedly too young to be hanging out alone in a diner at such a late hour. She was eating flan with obvious delight when another girl sat down at her table without even a word of greeting.

"Did you really have to call me so late...? It was a pain in the neck to leave undetected."

The newly arrived girl was a blond beauty, with her hair tied in two pigtails.

"You better have a good reason, or I'm going to be so mad at you. Oh, and you're paying, right?"

"Yeah. Order anything you like."

"Yay."

The blond girl picked up the menu and began to study it.

"Ryuunosuke Dazai doesn't know you're meeting me here, right?"

"Nah. Why stress him?"

"So it's just you and me, and nobody knows? Are you seriously so reckless? Or are you stupid? We're not at school. I could just kill you now."

"If you wanted to kill me, you'd have already done so, no? I'm still alive, which means your organization doesn't see me as a person of any importance. I'm perfectly safe."

"You shouldn't feel safe around me. Urgh, you get on my nerves... Anyway, what did you want?"

"Can't you guess?" The young-looking girl paused. "I work for the Calamity Research Institute. You're a mythical girl affiliated with the Order. We're enemies. What could I possibly want from you?"

"...Are you going to tell me, or what?"

The young girl finished her flan and sat up straighter, her face serious.

"I'd like to talk to you about the worst-case scenario."

◆

She was having an absurd dream. She was in a prison cell, alone. She knew she had to die. It didn't make sense, but it was her unavoidable fate.

"If I live, many people will die. Many already call for my death. They consider it the best option."

A wave of anger welled up in her body, threatening to take over. The rage inside her had a voice. It was the voice of her devil.

"How ridiculous! How illogical! A world in which there is no place for me, a world that is hostile to me, deserves to be destroyed."

The angry voice kept talking to her. She wasn't sure why she was feeling angry, too. Maybe she was railing at the injustice of her situation.

"But I am kind; I am merciful. I cannot bring myself to destroy the world in which he lives."

The thought of destroying it all, of burning everything down to the ground, was so sweet, though. Each act of destruction made that heavy feeling in her chest diminish. The ravaging flames cleared the fog in her head.

"For my own sake, I must kill him. Then I will destroy the world."

The devil's voice would not be quiet.

◆

"Ah…! It was…a dream…"

Rinne woke up from a nightmare in the middle of the night. She felt chilled to the bone but was drenched in sweat. Her heart was pounding, she was out of breath, and she couldn't focus her eyes for a while, at least until she became conscious of the calming smell of the boy sleeping with his back to her on the narrow futon next to hers. He was so close, she could feel the warmth radiating from his body. A familial warmth.

The girl had no memories of her family. Mythical girls had one more secret the boy didn't know about—they lost all memories of their life from before their mythical factor manifested. For this girl, that was ten years earlier. She couldn't remember a single thing before then, and she had spent the last decade shut inside the Calamity Research Institute's facility in a solitary prison cell. She had been suffering from terrible loneliness. But that was no more.

"I protected you because I wanted to."

She thought back to what Ryuunosuke had said to her that night and felt calm again. He'd said that without thinking, but to her, his words had monumental meaning. In the eyes of most humans, with her insane power, she was a monster they'd want nothing to do with. But that one boy wanted to save her, even at the cost of his own life. That act of kindness sufficed to make her fall in love with him.

"Ryuunosuke…"

Before him, she had never known love, so at first, she wasn't sure if that was what she was feeling. Her reaction to him was so strong, though, that she understood it couldn't be anything else.

She slipped under his covers and lay next to him. If she reached out to touch his back, she would feel his warmth directly. She was thinking about how he had shielded her with his body back then.

"Are you awake, Ryuunosuke...?" she whispered.

He didn't respond. She wanted to put her arm around him but hesitated. She craved so much to hold him, but her love for him made her fear his reaction. She knew she could not embrace him without holding back, or he'd die. To a dragon, human bodies were all too fragile.

The girl always had to hold back so that she wouldn't hurt anyone. That was just a fact of life for mythical girls.

"Tell me, Ryuunosuke..."

There was this one question always coming back to her when she was alone.

"...do you think some people do not deserve to live?"

She'd asked herself that question thousands of times. Now she posed it to the person she loved the most in the world. She'd never asked anyone else for their opinion.

She received no reply.

CHAPTER 4

The Mad Oracle of Gjallarhorn

Someone was there, in that dark room, shaking with ecstasy.

"Yes! Success!"

Their ring finger glowed red.

"Thanks to that boy, my research has finally yielded results after all these years…! My greatest wish is fulfilled at last! It's a miracle! No, it's destiny!"

They lifted their head as if to look at the sky, or maybe as an expression of bliss, as if they had just received an engagement ring from their beloved.

"Ha-ha-ha-ha-ha! I don't need that annoying girl anymore! Or that pesky vampire!"

They couldn't stop laughing maniacally, having succeeded where all others had failed.

"I will be the one to bring salvation to the world…"

The reflection of the ring shone in their eyes alongside euphoria… and madness.

"…by remaking it to suit me!"

◆

She hated uniforms—the forced conformity. A few months earlier, not long after cherry trees dropped their blossoms, she arrived at her new school just as the new school year started.

Her name was Mari Vlad Abara, fifteen years old. Her dad was Romanian, her mother Japanese. She had a sister several years younger than her. She was born in Bucharest and lived in Romania until she turned seven, when her family moved to Japan. Currently, she was living alone while her mom and dad worked abroad, her sister staying with them. She was in her first year of high school.

"Nice to meet you, everyone!"

She introduced herself to her classmates with a big smile. Everything she had just told them about herself was a lie.

Mari Vlad Abara wasn't a student, and all she knew about herself was that she was a world-class beauty and possessed the power of the vampire factor. Posing as a student, she had been tasked with monitoring the activities of the West Kokonoe branch of the Calamity Research Institute, and with capturing the Third Factor mythical girl. After she accomplished that, she would be assigned a new task.

It was always like this. There was the preparation stage and the action stage. Standard fare. She'd be spending her energy on yet another mission in the unending conflict between the Order and the Calamity Research Institute as her own execution inevitably approached.

In this worthless, rotten world where the mere fact that she existed was seen as a transgression, she had only this brief period leading up to her death to have a taste of what life was. Normal humans didn't have to live like this—which must have meant she wasn't human. That's the conclusion she'd arrived at.

She liked uniforms, because a uniform dress code was the perfect background against which to express her individuality.

Sitting in the last row next to the window with her chin resting in her hand, Mari absentmindedly stared at the world outside.

"What even is the point...? I'd be happier with everyone dead," she muttered.

She wasn't human, but she lived among humans, pretending to be one of them. It was so comical, it was tragic. She had to do it for her mission, but this strategy didn't seem effective to her. There was no better cover for her in this country than posing as a student; that was a fact, but she didn't like it.

Mari never dreamed about living an ordinary life. To her, her life was already over the moment the Order came to get her from a small orphanage in some insignificant little country when she began to express mythical girl abilities.

"This isn't a world for me. I'm like a fish out of water, being forced to live among land animals. It just won't work."

But even though she moaned about it, there was a part of her that enjoyed the novelty of school life. She just didn't want to admit it, even to herself.

School wasn't like the Order's training facility. At school, she was surrounded by normal people. Within the school walls, she lived like them.

And then she met him.

A few days after Mari transferred to the school…

"It's gone."

She'd just returned to her classroom after a lecture from her earnest teacher about how she should make more effort to fit in. The first-years' floor was deserted—everyone else had already gone home or to their school clubrooms. The orange-tinged sun was low on the horizon.

Before going to see her teacher, Mari had left her schoolbag on her desk, but when she returned to the classroom, it wasn't there.

"I don't think anyone would've taken it by mistake…"

She'd put a key chain on her bag with a toy that looked like someone's grossly mistaken idea of a rabbit. She'd gotten it from a capsule machine at the arcade near the train station. It was unlikely that another student would've taken her bag by mistake, and if they did, then their bag would've been left somewhere in the classroom.

Mari had an idea of what had happened.

"Those ugly bitches…"

The faces of three girls from her class flashed through her head. They were part of a group at the top of the school hierarchy. Mari had gotten an invite from them on her first day, but she refused, and for that "offense," she became a target for bullying. They'd talk crap about her looks just loud enough for her to hear. Now it seemed they'd escalated their bullying to stealing her stuff.

"Argh, what a pain. When you're pretty like me, you make enemies wherever you go."

She'd been ignoring her bullies when all they were doing was saying mean things about her. They were just weak humans, jealous because she was prettier than them. Taking her stuff, though, was too much to turn a blind eye to.

Mari went out into the hallway.

"What the...?"

The moment she stepped out of the classroom, she got an intense head rush. The world spun in front of her eyes, her mind fogged up, and she was so dizzy, she had to sit down.

"Ungh... Nnh..."

The symptoms resembled those of anemia, but Mari knew it wasn't that. It was her vampiric urges awakening. Soon enough, she was overcome with bloodlust, which felt like simultaneous hunger and thirst.

"No way..."

Mari pressed her hands to her chest, her eyes widened.

The vampire factor was ranked higher than the other factors, and it wasn't just because of the vampire mythical girls' useful ability to manipulate blood, auto-regeneration, or superior mobility. The main reason was that it was a very stable factor, predictably degenerating into the berserk status over time, but not at random. The vampiric urges were the only real drawback, but they were easy enough to suppress through regular consumption of blood. That day, as usual, Mari went to the rooftop after lunch to have her pouch of medical blood, but for some reason, it hadn't satisfied her bloodthirst. She had an extra pouch of blood just in case, of course, but it was in her schoolbag.

"This is…the worst timing…"

The vampiric urges couldn't be overcome through sheer will. Unlike thirst or hunger, they weren't urges of the body, but of the soul. And Mari had never felt bloodthirst this strong before. She could deal with it by drinking somebody's blood, but she could hardly do that without revealing she was a mythical girl, and the Order might execute her for letting that secret out. Mari wouldn't do that for another, more personal reason, too.

"Drinking some random human's blood…is totally gross."

The idea of indiscriminate feeding on any human she could get her hands on was repulsive to Mari. Historically, there had been mythical girls who did that. Mari thought of them as barbarians.

"Oof… Uh…"

She felt cold sweat on her back.

"Hey, are you okay?" someone asked her.

She was almost seeing double, but she turned toward the voice and saw a boy. His face seemed familiar. She recognized him as the student council member with an old-fashioned name. Even though he might be relatively well-known for his role on the student council, to Mari, he was like a generic background character. For reasons unknown, his clothes were all wet, his face was covered in bruises and scratches, and he was carrying a schoolbag with that ugly excuse for a rabbit key chain—it was Mari's bag.

"I was just searching for you. You're Abara, the first-year? You're not looking too good, if I'm to be honest. Should I walk you to the nurse office?"

It made her sick to hear that this dude knew her name. She just wanted him to leave her alone. If she wasn't feeling so out of it, she would've told him rudely to get lost.

"Uh...? Why're you...soaked...? What do you...want...?"

She wasn't even in a state to talk. The boy was concerned about her, which she found humiliating.

"I'm the vice president of the student council, in my second year here. The name's Ryuunosuke Dazai. Let me help you stand up."

He extended his hand to her.

"Whoa, your hand's ice-cold! Are you not well enough to stand? Hmm, piggyback won't work, from the look of things. Sorry, your clothes may get a bit wet."

Without waiting for her answer, Ryuunosuke put one arm around her torso and another under her knees.

"Hup!"

He lifted her up.

Being carried like a bride by this random guy was even more humiliating for Mari. She thought angrily that having a weakling like him carry her made her look heavy. At the same time, she felt her bloodlust grow in intensity. She looked at his neck—not too thick, not too thin. She wanted to sink her teeth into it so badly, it was driving her crazy. His smell made her salivate.

"The nurse isn't in..."

He carried her into the nurse's office and put her down on an empty bed.

"Give me...my bag..."

She took her bag from him and opened it with shaking hands.

"It's not there..."

Quite a few items were missing from her bag. The spare blood pouch looked like a squeezy juice pouch, so nobody would think it suspicious, but losing it was a problem.

"Something missing from your bag? I could go look for it."

"No... I'm...anemic. Just...leave me here..."

"What? No way. You're a first-year student; I'm your senior! You can rely on me. I'll stay with you until the nurse gets back."

She wanted to tell him to mind his own business.

"How did you know...it was my bag?"

"Huh? Ah, right. It's this weird rabbit key chain. Never seen anyone else with one like that."

"You're a creep...who goes around...checking out younger girl's bags?"

"No, but you stand out from the crowd, so I noticed. I randomly walked in on these girls trying to throw it into the pool. I guessed at once that they were bullies and jumped in, catching your bag in midair! I saved your bag, but I fell into the pool. That's why I'm wet, and why I had your bag."

"And why are you bruised?"

"The bullies called their boyfriends, who are a year older than me. We got in a scuffle. I know I look like I got a real bad beating, but they were the losers. I picked them up one by one and threw them into the pool. The girls, too. I bet they won't bully you again after that. But if they do try something funny, let me know, and I'll take care of it."

He laughed, then sneezed loudly.

"Achoo! Uh, feeling kinda cold after that unplanned swim."

Mari understood then that this boy was an idiot. There was still one thing she didn't get, though.

"Why did you...help me?"

"Why...? What?"

"You had no reason to do any of that..."

"Why would I need a reason?"

Mari saw pure honesty in his eyes.

"I helped you because I wanted to. I don't need a reason to help people."

Nobody else had ever said anything like that to Mari. She'd never had anyone go out of their way to help her, nor had she ever done that for anyone else. There had been no room in her life for random acts of kindness.

Ryuunosuke's words and sincere smile became permanently burned into her memory.

"You go to the trouble for nothing..."

"I don't see it as trouble. You're lucky I was in the right place at the right time!"

A sensation like an electric shock went through Mari's brain as the realization hit her that she wouldn't mind sucking his blood. It was an instinctive, not logical decision.

Everyone in the world was her enemy, or so she used to think. She had to keep living in that world, all alone. Ryuunosuke changed her thinking, though. When she imagined him becoming her only ally in this crappy world, everything went white in front of her eyes.

"...Nngh..."

She lost consciousness—that's how strong her bloodlust had grown.

"Ugh... Nnn..."

She came to not long after. Her thirst was still tormenting her. She looked around and saw Ryuunosuke had fallen asleep in his chair, resting his head on a table. The nurse must have been taking her time coming back to her office.

A few items were laid out on the desk next to Ryuunosuke—Mari's blood pouch, and other things that had been missing from her bag. Not that she cared at that moment.

The last rays of the setting sun were shining into the nurse's office. Mari could hear the school brass band having a rehearsal, and shouts from the gymnasium. She was alone with Ryuunosuke, and she couldn't take her eyes off his neck. He was so exposed, defenseless. So naive.

Mari's self-restraint reached its limits. She wanted his blood; she wanted it so bad. The thirst overpowered her.

She walked over to Ryuunosuke on unsteady feet, like a ghost in a horror flick. She didn't even spare the blood pouch a glance. Drinking the boy's blood was too risky; she shouldn't do it—but she wasn't thinking logically anymore. She had given in to her instincts.

"Huff... Huff..."

Her desires drowned out all rational thought.

"You want me to rely on you, you said. Fine, Mr. Upperclassman, I'll have you help me..."

She bit into the neck of this boy she had never spoken to before that day. He'd feel no pain, she knew. Vampire saliva contained a substance similar to morphine. If he woke up before she was finished, he might even feel pleasure. He didn't wake up, though, which was the best for both of them—if he had awoken, Mari would have to kill him.

For the first time in her life, she was sucking another person's blood. The sensation of warm blood filling her mouth was electrifying.

It was just so good.

She saw sparks, feeling as if her brain was buzzing with electricity. The rich aroma of the blood made her heady. Blood wasn't supposed to have sweetness to it, or umami, but that's how it tasted to Mari. For some reason, it had both an intoxicating and an energizing effect on her. In comparison, the medical blood for transfusions the Order gave her to drink was like watered-down milk.

She sucked Ryuunosuke's blood ravenously, lapping it up with delight, reveling in the elation it brought her.

After a while, she realized her bloodthirst had faded away.

"Mmm..."

She let go, satisfied, and the punctures on Ryuunosuke's neck closed immediately, thanks to another component of vampire saliva that stopped bleeding as soon as the vampire withdrew their fangs. Mari took out a handkerchief from her pocket and wiped both her mouth and Ryuunosuke's neck.

"Thank you for the lovely meal," she whispered into Ryuunosuke's ear as he slept.

After that, Mari packed her things into her bag and left the nurse's office.

The light of the setting sun illuminated her with its red glow. She felt happy, and there was a lightness in her step.

"Ryuunosuke Dazai," she repeated the boy's name to herself. "What a weird name."

For the first time in her life, she was interested in a boy. The fish out of water suddenly longed to live on land.

She wondered about Ryuunosuke's personality, his likes and dislikes, what he did after school, whether he would like her. Her curiosity

had been piqued and couldn't be suppressed. The emotions she was experiencing were so unfamiliar.

"He's on the student council..."

She thought that if she joined the council, too, she'd have the chance to get to know Ryuunosuke better.

"The student council president is that girl from the Calamity Research Institute. I don't know why she's posing as a student here, but I bet she already knows about me. She'd probably want to make contact with me anyway, so I'll ask her to sign me up for this council. It's up to me to make the first step!"

The next day, Mari noticed that her classmates were no longer interested in bullying her. Ryuunosuke wasn't at school that day—he stayed home with a cold.

It didn't take long for Mari to figure out what she was feeling toward Ryuunosuke.

◆

Mari yawned, waking up from that dream. She sleepily turned her head to look around. She was in the living room of a condo—one of the Order's safe houses in Kokonoe City.

It had been about two weeks since the girl with the dragon factor met the boy who possessed a Sacred Sealing Ring.

That morning, Mari had been unexpectedly called in to report to her superiors. She had arrived quite a bit early. The room where she was currently waiting was furnished only with a sofa, table, and chairs, arranged without any taste for interior design. There wasn't even a rug on the floor. She had stretched out on the sofa when she got there early in the morning, then nodded off, dreaming about her first meeting with Ryuunosuke two months earlier.

"Tee-hee..."

She couldn't help smiling at the thought of Ryuunosuke. Meeting him was truly life-changing for her. He was her first love. She'd never tried to get anyone to fall in love with her, either. Every day, she went to school excited about what might happen, wishing that things could stay like that forever.

"I'm getting sentimental..."

Would she be executed after going berserk, or just before it happened? In any case, death awaited her in the not-too-far future. She'd accepted that, but surely, she should be allowed to at least enjoy the brief time she had until then?

Ryuunosuke gave her hope. With his power, he might be able to postpone her eventual execution or maybe even save her from it. To any mythical girl, he was the miraculous ray of hope, the coveted chance of salvation.

Out of concern for Ryuunosuke, Mari committed an act of treason against her organization—she didn't report that he was a soul linker with a Sacred Sealing Ring. She supposed he'd happily soul link with her if she asked him, but then the Order might demand his capture. So she didn't ask.

She'd face repercussions once the Order discovered what she'd done, but she didn't care.

"So I'm stuck sitting on this fence... Come on, Mari, you have to commit to one side or the other..."

She chuckled wryly, and just then, she heard the front door unlock and open. She sensed the presence of a person and heard one pair of footsteps. Guarded, perhaps unnecessarily, she waited for the visitor to come to the living room.

It was the man known as Loki, who spied for the Order by working undercover at the Calamity Research Institute. Mari didn't really know anything about him besides his fake name. She didn't really get along with him. In fact, she could barely stand him.

"Whew."

Loki plopped down on a chair.

"Good morning, Marie."

"Don't call me that."

She didn't like just anyone referring to her by that nickname. There were very few people at the Order whom she allowed to use it, and Loki wasn't one of them. She absolutely hated him calling her "Marie."

"Where are the others?" asked Mari.

"Don't ask me. Maybe they'll come later."

"Whatever. Why was I asked to report in all of a sudden?"

"Because there's been a change, and you're required to check in with another research facility. You were assigned here to capture the dragon factor girl, and that task has now been voided."

"Did you do something to her?"

"Oh no, no. It seems the CRI is one step ahead of us, based on how they equipped the dragon factor girl with her Valkyrie Suit before transporting her, as if they knew what we were going to try. Well, enough about that. You have new orders."

Loki paused for a moment.

"Mari Vlad Abara, you are removed from this operation. Return to Yokone Base."

"What?" Mari shouted in protest. "I'm being ordered to return there?! Why?!"

"Because that's what you're being ordered to do, simple."

"Who decided this?! I...don't want leave yet..." Mari riled at the sudden change of assignment, thinking about Ryuunosuke—her first love.

"Well, this is funny. You kicked up such a fuss about going undercover as a student. Don't tell me you started to actually enjoy school life?"

"It's not about that. I just think the reassignment doesn't make sense..."

"Orders are orders. You don't get to have your say. Be a good girl and do as you're told."

"I don't understand the reason for forcing me to abandon this mission!"

Loki covered his face with his right hand and sighed loudly. He moved his hair out of the way, spread out his fingers, and peered at Mari from in between them.

"Stop yapping, you annoying bitch."

His voice had suddenly changed, becoming cold and filled with hatred. "Are you stupid? I'm not asking you nicely to 'pretty please' do this; I'm giving you your orders. You say, 'Yes, sir, understood,' not argue with me. The Order owns you, and you do as you're told. Or do you have trouble comprehending? We're acting for the greater good of all humanity, and you? You are like a disease plaguing humanity. You don't even deserve to live. Don't think for a moment you get to have a say about what happens to you."

"You bastard!"

Mari sprang to her feet.

"Oh? Want to fight?"

"And what if I do?"

"You really are mentally challenged. You can't change your orders by acting up."

"That's what you say. But maybe this will get the higher-ups to reconsider."

"Have it your way."

Loki stood up from his chair and raised his right hand.

"You're beyond help."

A red ring of light appeared around Loki's ring finger. Mari had seen one like that before.

"You have...a Sacred Sealing Ring?!"

The color and position on the finger were slightly different from Ryuunosuke's, but as a mythical girl, Mari could immediately tell it was a real Sacred Sealing Ring. In response to it, the Stigma on her chest lit up, and she lost all her strength. Loki grabbed her by her hair and pushed her face down onto the floor.

"Argh...?! I...can't...move?!"

No ordinary human, no matter how strong, could rival a mythical girl, but Loki was totally overwhelming her thanks to the power of the ring.

"How did you...get that ring...?"

"Why would I tell you? By the way, I know you didn't report that brat had one, to protect him."

"..."

Surprised both by the sudden orders to return to the base and Loki being in possession of a Sacred Sealing Ring, Mari was struck by realization that at the Order she was just a pawn, oblivious to the greater picture.

"Well, anyway, it doesn't matter. But get it into your thick head that I can kill you anytime. You're allowed to live only as long as you walk nicely on a leash, and even that wouldn't be the case if you weren't third rank."

Still holding her by her hair, Loki pressed her face harder against the floor.

"I don't have patience for disobedient trash like you. The fact that you're just a stupid kid doesn't earn you any sympathy points with me when you throw a temper tantrum. Your schoolgirl act is over, so go back to the base and don't ever talk back to me again."

"..."

"There's less than twenty-four hours remaining. Now that I've tested the ring, it's time to move on to the final step."

Mari had no choice but to obey her orders. She'd always done as the Order commanded. She'd only been faking being a schoolgirl as part of her mission anyway. Orders had to be carried out to the letter. The alternative was most likely death. Going back to the base just meant resuming her normal life.

And yet she couldn't stop thinking about the boy she'd fallen in love with.

Loki smiled thinly.

"I am the messiah. The world is saved."

◆

Two weeks since meeting Ryuunosuke, Rinne had gotten acclimatized to school life. She made friends and was enjoying the same normal life as her schoolmates. Meanwhile, Ryuunosuke became so used to her being a part of his life that it didn't even occur to him to imagine it changing.

"She did not come to school today," Rinne said to Ryuunosuke as they were leaving the school building.

"Huh?"

Ryuunosuke didn't immediately realize she was talking about Mari.

Mari had missed her classes that day, and she didn't show up in the student council room, either. Without her radiance, the room had seemed darker than usual to Ryuunosuke.

"I guess sometimes, she can't come in. She's got a lot going on, too," he said, not really worried.

"I suppose so," Rinne replied stiffly.

Recently, Rinne would sometimes fall into a gloomy mood, but Ryuunosuke felt they hadn't been friends long enough for him to ask her about it outright.

They suddenly stopped. Two black armored cars were parked just outside the school gates. Ryuunosuke didn't know anything about car makes, but he could tell immediately that those were pretty expensive vehicles.

Outside the black cars stood men in black suits. Ryuunosuke guessed they were from the Calamity Research Institute's Section One, which was an experimental but fully operational unit focusing on finding military applications for mythical factor powers. They were the main force deployed for armed conflicts. Tough-looking Section One members would sometimes escort Ryuunosuke and Rinne to their checkups, but Ryuunosuke hadn't really had much contact with them.

"Huh, what's that about...?" he said.

He didn't find it alarming that the Section One guys were waiting for them but thought it odd that three of them had come to pick them up, bringing two cars. Normally, it was just one person and one car.

"You're out in full force today, Mr. Yanagida?" He greeted a big, bearlike man he recognized.

"The plan's a bit different today. Only Rinne Irako is going in for her medical."

Rinne cocked her head at him.

"Why?"

"We haven't been told the details."

"I'm not coming with her?"

"No. These two guys will escort you to your house, where you are to wait for Rinne's return."

"Okay, got it."

Ryuunosuke readily agreed, assuming the Calamity Research Institute had its reasons, but Rinne pouted, unhappy with this arrangement.

"Get in the cars, kids."

"No. I refuse to go anywhere without Ryuunosuke."

"Sorry, but this time—"

"I am not going anywhere without Ryuunosuke."

"We've been ordered to escort him home, though..."

"Whose orders are these?"

"Deputy Chief Researcher Akeda's, I'm told."

"Ranko decided this...?" Rinne said quietly to herself. "I cannot conceive why she would give you such orders."

"Come now, don't make our job difficult."

"Let me speak with Ranko."

"The underground facility is completely cut off to preserve its secrecy. Well, there are ways to get in touch with the staff there, but I'm not authorized to do this."

"Tsk... I do not want to go without speaking to Ranko..."

"Rinne, come on. Let's not drag this out," Ryuunosuke cut in.

Yanagida had given him a look, which he read as a request for help.

"Why should I go alone? When you and I are together, we are safe. You should be close to me in case something was to happen to me. This is the basic stipulation of the Dragon Babysitter Project."

"That's all true, but it looks like this time, Ranko needs only you to come in. I'm sure it'll be fine."

"No, Ryuunosuke—"

"Let's not make it difficult for everyone—"

"Does 'everyone' include you?" Rinne snapped at him. She instantly regretted it. "I'm sorry for speaking in anger. I became emotional, because to me, you are…"

She fell silent, closing her eyes for a moment.

"Tell me, Ryuunosuke, do you not want me to be with you? Am I a bother?"

"Whoa, whoa! Where's this come from?"

"I am… I am a bother to you after all, am I not?" she said in a voice trembling from emotion.

"That night, when I asked you…"

Rinne's eyes suddenly opened wider as if in sudden realization, and she froze.

"What night? Asked me wha—?"

"I will go alone," she cut him off.

◆

Ryuunosuke got a ride home, where he was ordered to wait for Rinne. He didn't really have anything to do that evening, so he just lay down.

"Hmm…"

Yanagida and another Section One member called Kuroi were standing guard outside his front door. Ryuunosuke had met both during earlier pickups.

The boy had tried to convince Rinne to go along with the orders so as not to get her or the Section One guys in trouble, but it was as if they'd been on different wavelengths.

"What was she going to say…?"

She had asked him something one night, apparently, and it seemed very important to her, but she couldn't bring herself to talk about it.

"Come to think of it…I don't see a reason why she should go in alone, either."

The ring's effects weakened the greater the distance between him and Rinne, which was the reason they should stick close. It was strange that Ranko would ask only Rinne to come in, but maybe it was for some experiment. Without knowing the details, all Ryuunosuke could do was guess the reasoning. He did have this funny feeling nagging at him, but he could hardly oppose the grown-ups sent from the facility based on a vague feeling something wasn't right. He was just a student, after all. He doubted he had any say in what the Calamity Research Institute could do to him and Rinne.

"Ranko would've explained what was up... Yanagida said she gave the orders, but somehow, I don't think it was her..."

Maybe he was wrong. Or maybe the orders came from someone even higher up than Ranko. He had a feeling someone other than Ranko was behind the change in routine, but at that point, there wasn't anything he could do anyway.

He was growing worried about Rinne.

"...I shouldn't have told her to go."

Ryuunosuke rolled onto his other side.

Rinne was single-mindedly in love with him. He used her feelings for him to have her comply with the orders, without hearing out her concerns.

I'll have to apologize to her when she's back...

He took his phone out of his pocket, opened the browser app, and navigated to the news site he'd been checking regularly since stumbling on it two weeks earlier. The headline about the convicted murderer being sentenced to death was still in the hot-topics column.

"Oh, wait..."

Ryuunosuke made the connection and broke out into a cold sweat, realizing what question had been eating up Rinne. He remembered her asking him, one night...

"Do you think some people do not deserve to live?"

◆

Yanagida, who'd been in the Japan Self-Defense Force before joining the Calamity Research Institute's Section One, was also mulling over that night's orders with growing suspicion.

"Hmm…," he muttered, stroking his chin.

"Thinking hard about something, Mr. Yanagida?" asked Kuroi, standing guard next to him.

Kuroi was ex-police. He'd joined the Calamity Research Institute only recently, so Yanagida hadn't gotten much of an insight into his personality yet, but he knew the man was sharp and serious.

"Something bugging you about this mission?" Kuroi asked.

"You can tell?"

"With how much you've been groaning under your breath, yeah."

"No matter how much I think about it, it doesn't make sense."

"Care to explain?"

"This kid, he's participating in some CRI research project. Why would he need us guarding him? If the CRI thought he was in any danger, two of us don't stand a chance against the Order's Kampfers or mythical girls. And if it's not the Order he has to be protected against, that's a job for the police, not us."

The lower the rank one held in an organization's hierarchy, the less information was shared—that wasn't anything unusual. Yanagida didn't know about Ryuunosuke's ring, for example. His orders were to guard the boy, without any supplementary information.

"And who is this boy, really? The CRI contacted him after the events following the Order's attack on our transport. Is this high school student really that important? If he is and needs to be guarded from something, he'd be safer just going to the CRI together with Irako. I don't understand why they'd split up him and the mythical girl."

"The answer's pretty simple," Kuroi said, pointing up with his index finger.

"If he was with the mythical girl, it'd be that much harder to kill him."

＊　　＊　　＊

It took a moment for Yanagida to process what he'd just heard.

"You're a spy—"

Yanagida reached for his automatic rifle, but Kuroi got him first with his 9mm handgun.

◆

Ryuunosuke heard a loud popping sound right outside his house.

"Run away!" Yanagida shouted.

Then there was another popping sound. This time, Ryuunosuke knew right away it was gunfire. He thought about escape routes. He didn't have many options in his cramped little house. The bathroom and toilet windows were out of the question—they were close to the front door and too small anyway. The west- and east-facing windows of the living room were also too close to the front of the house. This left the north-facing window in his bedroom—or currently, Ranko's room—which was on the rear side of the house.

Ryuunosuke was simultaneously thinking about the CRI men.

Was it them who got shot, or did they shoot someone else? Is Mr. Kuroi okay?! Do I go help them or run away?

Ryuunosuke was just a high schooler. There was no way he could do any good in a situation where military-trained men were firing guns at one another. Despite that, he pondered whether to run or get help until it was too late. Kuroi kicked the front door off its hinges and burst into the house.

Wait, did Mr. Kuroi shoot Mr. Yanagida?!

It didn't make sense, but it sure seemed that way. The hallway lead straight into the living room. Ryuunosuke was in range.

Kuroi raised his weapon and fired. Ryuunosuke rolled to dodge the shot. The bullet flew above his head, piercing the sliding door behind him.

Kuroi was now in the living room.

"Mr. Kuroi, stop! Why are you—?"

But instead of replying, Kuroi took aim at the boy.

It was painfully clear that Ryuunosuke's experience in martial arts, weight training, and victories in fights with other school kids weren't the least bit helpful in this situation.

I'm a hopeless idiot. She was right; we should have stayed together. She was risking getting in trouble to protect me, and I stupidly insisted she should go alone. Forgive me, Rinne...

The gun fired with a ruthlessly cold, dry *pop*, pronouncing the end to the boy's short life.

◆

Meanwhile, Rinne was in Lab Room Number Five at the Underground Kokonoe Factor Research Facility. The room was a sterile white. It was clean, but various research implements were strewed about. Rinne had been in that room many times, and its medical smell was familiar to her.

She was sitting in a chair near the automatic door, opposite Suberu Sarashina, who was dressed in his white lab coat. He was carrying out the routine medical checks on her that day. Rinne showed him her arm, and he stuck the needle of a syringe into her vein. When she wasn't expressing her factor powers, Rinne had normal human skin, which could be easily pierced with a needle.

Why did I have to say those things to him...?

Rinne deeply regretted her immaturity, shouting emotionally at Ryuunosuke like a little girl having a tantrum. He didn't say anything wrong. If the orders were for her to come for her checks alone, she should just do that unquestioningly. She wanted to live like any other normal human, so why did she kick up such a fuss over something that was perfectly normal just because of her vague unease? Ryuunosuke was only trying to make her act sensibly, no doubt worried that the childish display would get both her and the Section One men in trouble. She knew that, so why did she make it about something else?

One evening, she'd seen a comment about something entirely unrelated to her on Ryuunosuke's phone. A comment saying some people didn't deserve to live. It was just a thoughtless message written by some site user, but it stuck with Rinne, constantly sneaking into her thoughts.

Even if the whole world thought her existence was unnecessary, she wanted at least Ryuunosuke to need her. When he told her not to make things difficult for everyone, it triggered her internal anxiety about being an unwelcome presence to him, and she desperately wanted him to reassure her that wasn't the case. She didn't want to be taken away from him.

I will sincerely apologize to him later...

"Everything seems within the norm," Suberu said, entering data on a tablet after giving Rinne the injection. "To think an unstable Third Factor in an autophagic state could be completely restored to normal... It must be the effect of the world-saving light, I suppose."

"What do you mean?"

"Light at a very special frequency, which only those qualified to become the messiah are able to absorb."

"...I do not follow."

"The light doesn't only suppress the devil but can kill it, too."

Rinne felt a growing unease, as Suberu seemed to be talking not to her, but to himself about something really strange. She decided to change the topic.

"May I ask you a question?"

"What is it?"

Sarashina smiled at her broadly.

"Why was I asked to come in without Ryuunosuke today? It seems illogical to me."

"I'm afraid I don't know."

"And why are you examining me today instead of Ranko?"

"I'm afraid I don't know."

"A couple weeks ago, Ryuunosuke slipped and mentioned his Sacred Sealing Ring when you were driving us to the facility. Why did you pretend you did not know about the ring?"

"..."

"You reacted as if you had no idea what ring Ryuunosuke was talking about. You might not have been told he was a soul linker, but as a mythical factor researcher, you would have certainly known about the Sacred Sealing Rings. Your reaction was very strange."

"Ah, well pointed out." Sarashina kept smiling just as before. "I will now answer all your questions."

Just as he was saying that, the world spun in front of Rinne's eyes.

"What…?"

The floor was approaching her at high speed. She felt her head crash into it. She didn't immediately understand that she'd fallen off the chair.

"I had been setting up the pieces for this project."

Rinne could see Suberu out of the corner of her eye. She couldn't see his face, though.

"I cannot…mo…"

She couldn't move at all.

"So as for my reaction to the mention of the ring, I admit I messed up. The dumb vampire failed to report that the boy had a Sacred Sealing Ring, so I was completely thrown and made up that lousy lie on the spot."

"She didn't report it…," Rinne whispered in a labored, hoarse voice, breathing shallowly.

"Also, sorry—the injection I gave you wasn't your usual solution for checkups. It was poison. Your Third Factor powers are strong beyond belief. I gave you enough poison to kill thousands of men, but you're just temporarily paralyzed, it seems."

Rinne finally realized how foolish she'd been.

I am a hopeless idiot. Had I truly loved Ryuunosuke with all my heart, I would have never left his side, even if he were to despise me for it. Forgive me… Forgive me, Ryuunosuke…

◆

The Order had a spy in the Calamity Research Institute.

"The rat is either in the research department or higher up."

Ranko Akeda was walking down the long hallways of the Underground Kokonoe Factor Research Facility in her white lab coat. For a while, she'd had a faint suspicion that there might be a spy in her organization. The attack on the helicopter transporting Rinne proved her suspicion correct.

The CRI planned the transport route so it would be extremely difficult to predict and follow, but the enemy knew exactly where the helicopter would be passing through and when. The only way they could have known that was through an informer at the CRI.

At first, Ranko's suspicions fell on Ryuunosuke Dazai, but she quickly ruled him out. His meeting with Rinne was purely coincidental, and he hadn't had any contact with the CRI before then.

There weren't many people who knew about Rinne's transport: the higher-ups in the ops team, and a handful of staff from their special forces and the research department.

The bosses of the other sections and the higher-ups had been slow to investigate this, so Ranko took the matters into her own hands, short-listing the suspects in her own department and removing them from her team.

There was a possibility the spy was among the higher-ups, but if that was the case, there'd be nothing Ranko could do about it. That's why she chose to act under the assumption that the spy was among the researchers.

"Hmm? Why am I the one looking for the spy...? It's not a job for a researcher, but for Section Two...," Ranko muttered to herself.

She stopped in front of Lab Room Number Five. The screen next to the automatic door showed a record of someone entering the room about half an hour earlier. Ranko guessed it was Rinne and Ryuunosuke. She thought about doing something to surprise them when she entered, but Ryuunosuke didn't take jokes well, and she didn't want him to assign her more house chores in retribution.

Rinne's outlook was positive. The stability of her factor was eye-opening for Ranko. Only two weeks earlier, Rinne was at berserk phase one, but she recovered without any trace of abnormalities. Degenerating into berserk status was previously thought irreversible, and the suppressants produced by the lab could only slow down the process.

The Sacred Sealing Rings, though, appeared to have the power to cure mythical girls who had gone berserk.

To Ranko, who'd long been researching the synthesis of artificial Sacred Sealing Rings, the sudden appearance of Ryuunosuke was a godsend. She didn't mind devoting her whole life if needed to erase all mythical factors from the world, ending the tragedy of mythical girls.

"If only I could ask him to soul link with all mythical girls already..."

She was garnering precious data from Ryuunosuke, but much remained unknown about the workings of the Sacred Sealing Rings. If Ryuunosuke could share the dragon factor's regenerative ability, there was a possibility he'd suffer negative effects by being linked with a mythical girl.

Ranko entered the code for the room and pressed her hand to a scanner, which checked her fingerprints. The door slid open.

"...Rinne?"

The first thing she noticed was that Rinne was on the floor, in the middle of that white-walled lab that resembled a hospital room, with computers and other research devices and implements all around. Ranko was so shocked that she realized after a delay that there was another person in the room—Suberu Sarashina.

"What are you do—?"

She was cut off by the bang of his gun. He shot her in the stomach. The dull pain from the shot wound didn't come instantly.

Ranko fell backward, hitting the door that had closed behind her. With her back against it, she slowly slid to the floor, leaving a bloody smear.

The bullet didn't hit any vital organs, but she was in a critical condition nonetheless. Ranko pressed her left hand to the wound and glared at Suberu, trying to suppress the pain.

"...It was you."

Ranko had considered the possibility Suberu might be the rat. She was planning to temporarily move him to another research facility to test her suspicions—but she'd acted too late. His reassignment had already been registered in the system, which meant he'd lose access to Ranko's labs, but the security updates took twenty-four hours to be processed. Suberu had used that time to his advantage.

"Not only me," Suberu replied nonchalantly.

For some reason, he was wearing a white glove on his right hand, the one that was holding the gun.

"There are others in Section One and Section Three. I don't think of them as allies, though—just bribed pawns to be discarded after use."

Of course he had to have a helper in Section Three, the internal security. Otherwise, it wouldn't have been possible for him to bring a gun into the facility.

"You do realize this is pointless, don't you? Security will be here soon. You won't be able to escape," Ranko said solemnly.

"Don't worry about me, I've taken measures."

Suddenly, an alarm sounded. It was the third-degree emergency alert, used for major accidents at the facility. Even during evacuation drills, it was rarely used, and so predictably, it sent everyone into a state of panic. Whether the alarm had been activated by mistake or not, everyone had to leave the facility immediately and head to the shelter.

"The traitor in Section Three is behind this, huh... You've created a distraction, but it's only temporary. You won't leave this facility on your own terms."

"That's not a problem. I'm not planning on leaving."

"If your plan was to stay here, I'm afraid you've already ruined your chances of keeping this job."

But maybe he'd meant that he wasn't planning on making it out alive. Ranko had something else on her mind than chatting with Suberu, though—she was worried about Rinne.

"Rinne, are you alive?"

"I...am... Cannot...move... He gave me...a shot..."

"He must've mixed in factor suppressant..."

Of all factors, the dragon factor had the highest resistance to poison. Resistance didn't equal invulnerability, though. Even though the strongest of poisons might not be deadly to a dragon girl, she would still suffer from some of its effects. Rinne had been injected with a substance able to kill a human many times over, but Ranko reckoned she'd be able to neutralize the toxins in a matter of minutes, recovering from paralysis.

Naturally, Suberu must have known that, too. Ranko couldn't understand his objective, but she hoped to distract him long enough for Rinne to recover before he did something worse.

"Where's Dazai boy?"

"At home… Your orders…"

Ranko hadn't issued such orders. It became clear to her that Suberu had orchestrated this very carefully.

"What are you trying to achieve here?" she asked him.

"Save the world, obviously."

There was no hint of sarcasm in his voice.

"What…?" Ranko was thrown by this incongruous declaration. "Sorry?"

"I'm going to save the world. This generation of the dragon factor going berserk has the potential to cause cataclysmal damage. The dragon heart's explosion might well destroy the whole world. To put it simply, my plan is to detonate the bomb known as Rinne Irako and blow the world to pieces."

"I thought you were talking about saving the world, not destroying it. You're contradicting yourself."

"Not at all. To save it, I must destroy the world."

Ranko had to reevaluate him. Keeping the existence of mythical factors secret and supervising mythical girls to prevent them from destroying the world was a basic principle governing the actions of both the Calamity Research Institute and the Order. The two organizations were hostile to each other, but Ranko trusted the Order not to break that golden rule. She was convinced that the Order would never hatch a plan to use the dragon heart to destroy the planet. Which meant that her suspicions about Suberu were incorrect.

"You're not working for the Order…"

"Of course not." He confirmed her growing fears.

Ranko stared at him, bewildered. This was the least probable yet absolutely worst-case scenario.

"A pathetic organization like the Order isn't worthy of carrying out the glorious task of saving the world. That is a task for a true hero of humanity. Meaning me."

"That is what he meant in the car back then, when he said he was saving the world…," Rinne said quietly.

Suberu's eyes were sparkling.

"I'm a member of the Order, too, that's true. I've been making use of them as needed, but they were only a stepping stone for me. Their doctrine simply doesn't agree with mine."

"You're not acting on anyone's orders… You're executing your own plan…?"

"A plan informed by the world savior's wisdom, yes."

He wasn't making any sense. What Ranko garnered from his explanation was that he was a madman.

"In their arrogance, humans continue to fight among themselves, creating endless cycles of envy and rage… Even understanding this, they're too apathetic to take any action to break this cycle. Their greed can never be satisfied, only growing the more they consume, foolishly twisting their interpretation of reality to suit their needs. That's why the mythical girls, the enemies of humanity's prosperity, have appeared in the world. They're the mechanism of humanity's apoptosis; they're the original sin! But I—I shall free humanity from this sin once and for all!"

"If you see salvation in death, why don't you just kill yourself and spare us all the trouble of having to deal with you?"

"Your crude take on what I said is typical of human ignorance. It's so frustrating that people can't see the truth even when it's presented to them on a platter. It can't be helped, I suppose. I only stumbled on it by pure chance myself."

Suberu spread his arms wide and looked up, as if he could see the sky through the ceiling.

"We need not accept the astral plane–born autoimmune disorder of humanity as a curse we must live with. Cells cannot be protected from death by wrapping them in aluminum foil, but there is hope! The liquefied body of a caterpillar inside a chrysalis reconstitutes itself into a butterfly! It is not until an eggshell is cracked that you see whether it contains a chick inside! I know the truth, and so I must save the world! It falls to a human to destroy the mythical factors!"

The two girls were taken aback by the depth of Suberu's insanity. Ranko recovered from her speechlessness first.

"It's a reckless plan you have…and I can tell you it's also impossible. You can't force Rinne to go berserk."

"Because she's protected by the ring she's linked with, you mean?"

"So you know about Dazai boy's ring…"

All information related to Ryuunosuke's ring was strictly classified, and no staff who was ranked C or lower had access to it. That included Suberu.

"Did you get that information from the Order, through Abara…?"

"No, she didn't report it. I found out by a fortunate coincidence."

"What…?"

"I haven't notified the Order, either. Rest assured that they know nothing about you having a soul linker at your disposal."

"In any case, you should give up. Soul linking suppresses the devil inside mythical girls, stopping them from reaching even berserk phase one. Rinne won't be your world-destroying bomb."

"You're right in saying that she's protected from going berserk while she's soul linked. This is a simple problem to solve, though. She just needs to be unlinked."

"That's why you separated them… To kill Dazai boy…"

"Kill…Ryuunosuke…?"

Rinne couldn't move, but her rage was palpable in the air.

"Stay calm, Rinne. If he were dead, you'd have been unlinked and gone berserk already. As long as you have that ring on your finger, you know he's alive."

He might not be unharmed, but he wasn't dead, at least. There was hope for him. Ranko had more immediate danger to focus on.

"He should be dead by now, actually. I wonder what happened."
Suberu didn't seem to particularly care.

"Sarashina... Your plan is full of holes. You haven't thought this through properly, have you? You're relying too much on luck. I reckon your chances of success are close to nil."

"Killing the boy is only a secondary element of my plan. I decided on it to cover all the bases and eliminate the tiniest possibility of him relinking with Rinne."

"Wait, so killing him isn't how you intend to make Rinne berserk? But there is no other way..."

Ranko stopped, as a terrifying idea hit her. But that couldn't be; it wasn't realistically possible. But even as she denied it to herself, she saw that it was the answer making all the pieces fall into place. This was a scenario so bad and so improbable, she hadn't even considered it before.

What if Suberu had a Sacred Sealing Ring?

"I can read on your face that you finally figured it out. Yes, I have it."
Ranko felt a paralyzing dread. Suberu took off his white glove.

"Witness the radiance of the world savior's wisdom!"

At the base of Suberu's ring finger was a ring of red light.
"That...cannot be..."
"A Sacred Sealing Ring?!"

Rinne and Ranko stared in astonishment. The ring's color, shape, and position on the finger were a bit different from Ryuunosuke's.

"An inferior version of a Sacred Sealing Ring. You could call it a Synthetic Sealing Ring. I created this artifact not that long ago," Suberu said triumphantly.

"C-rank staff, stealing confidential research data... That's punishable by memory erasure. But even with my data—"

"'I shouldn't be able to succeed in producing the ring in a matter of two weeks'—is that what you were going to say?" He forestalled Ranko's question.

Both girls fell silent—they'd been thinking the same thing.

"The Order has made quite surprising advancements in their research of artificial factor generation, as well as Sacred Sealing Rings. But you know about this, don't you?"

"..."

"I solved the mysteries of the rings by combining my world savior's wisdom with the data you had on the boy's ring. With that information, producing the ring was simple enough."

Only staff with B-rank or higher authorization could access the research data on the ring. Ranko made a mental note that Suberu must have roped in someone very high up to aid him.

"The rings are composed of mythical ideas interfering with astral receptors, expressing the X factor through Id neuron network singularity. The answer was well within reach once you know what you're looking for."

Ranko used to consider Suberu a very talented researcher, but she had underestimated him. He was a bona fide genius. He might have become a great man of science, had he channeled his intellectual gifts in another direction.

"This Synthetic Sealing Ring is, as I said, an inferior version of the real rings. You might be familiar with the philosophical argument that a human cannot know what it is like to be a bat, because we are only capable of working within the framework of human concepts. This ring does not enable me to soul link with mythical girls to strengthen their factors or neutralize their berserk status. But that is of no importance—I do not need those powers."

"You have overlooked one problem...," Rinne said, still down on the floor but looking Suberu straight in the eyes.

"Oh, you seem to be feeling better. And what is it you believe I overlooked?"

"Your plan will not work, because I will kill you!"

She sprang up, having recovered from the effects of the poison to an extent, although her movements weren't as fast as normal. She aimed a brutal kick at Suberu's face...

"Stop."

*   *   *

She didn't manage to get him. His ring shone, and Rinne collapsed back onto the floor.

"My...Stigma..."

The Stigma reappeared on her chest, despite her having a Sacred Sealing Ring on her finger.

"No wonder mythical girls become so twisted—that's what happens when you give a kid power they don't deserve. Violence is wrong; why don't you understand...? But we will have peace again."

Suberu stared down at Rinne with contemptuous disgust, as if she were a crushed cockroach.

"You've been hoping to buy yourselves time until she recovered from the poison, haven't you? But in fact, I was the one who needed time. It seems the activation isn't immediate. Some conditions must be met first."

His ring and Rinne's mark were flickering, as if their powers were vying for supremacy.

"The synthetic ring is missing some of the functions of the original. What it can do, though, is weaken mythical girls and propel them toward going berserk."

He paused, relishing this slow, sinister reveal.

"It can also...cancel soul linking."

Rinne and Ranko went pale, sensing that he wasn't lying.

"The cost of delinking a mythical girl and making her berserk is the life and soul of the ring-wearer. Unfortunately, it is one demerit I could not excise from its functionality..."

"You're going to sacrifice yourself for this?" asked Ranko.

"Yes, but since the world will soon be destroyed, what does it matter? I would've died regardless. In the past, people would offer sacrifices during their demon-summoning rituals. If my sacrifice can save the world, I will gladly offer up my life... My only regret is that I won't be there to witness the completion of my project. Well, anyway... While I'm still here, let me tell you something, Third Factor girl. It's a funny little theory I've developed."

His cold smile betrayed a sadistic pleasure.

                                *   *   *

"Your feelings for Dazai are fake."

Rinne's eyes went wide.

"What…?"

"The Sacred Sealing Ring's soul linking mechanism strengthens the bond between mythical girls and the linker. One's soul and emotions are closely tied, and desire and love are the most powerful feelings bringing one soul closer to another. Based on this, it is highly possible that Dazai's ring manipulated your psyche to make you fall in love with him."

He paused before teasing Rinne more.

"Has this never crossed your mind? Haven't you thought it strange that you had fallen in love with a broke student in such a short amount of time? What an odd coincidence it would be to fall in love with your soul linker. No, it was the ring that created artificial feelings of love in your heart."

Rinne was staring at the floor, not saying anything.

"Well, what do you think? We have no way to test my theory, but hasn't it made you question your feelings? Doubt them? Your love for that boy is all you have—how sad for it to only be an illusion."

Suberu was clearly saying that just to be mean. A researcher, spinning his baseless theory to mentally torture a young girl—how odious.

"Heh…"

Rinne's reaction wasn't what he'd been expecting, though.

"Ha-ha-ha-ha-ha!" She laughed as if he'd told a good joke.

"…What's so funny?"

"Your 'little funny theory,' what else? You shared it with me for amusement, yet you are confused by getting a laugh?"

Rinne looked up at him. There were beads of sweat on her forehead, and she seemed to be overheating, but she was smiling defiantly.

"A funny theory indeed. My love for Ryuunosuke is a lie, you suggest. Hilarious. Even if it were, that matters not in the least," she said decisively. "Acting out of empathy to protect others even at the cost of sustaining injury, while having no illusions as to one's powerlessness…

Ryuunosuke possesses qualities of character that make him a suitable mate for me. There is no other man like him. And as for regards my feelings for him, there is nothing artificial about them."

She sucked in air like a dragon preparing to breathe fire.

"It is beyond doubt that my love for him is genuine!"

Ranko teared up at that. Mythical girls were cursed with a cruel fate, robbed of their youth. Rinne's short life had been riddled with hardships, yet in a very brief span of time, she had grown so strong. Perhaps she'd always been stronger than Ranko had thought.

The mocking smile vanished from Suberu's face.

"Well, unfortunately, the boy you love is going to die."

"No. He is alive, and he is not going to die."

"He may be alive now, but not for long. A schoolkid can't fight off a trained—"

"No. He is not. Going. To. Die," she interrupted him.

"Tsk!" Suberu clicked his tongue with frustration. "Hope is not for you. You don't belong in this world. You're cancer. You're a devil. It would violate the laws of the universe. A destructive factor nobody needs—which everybody wants to be excised from our world—daring to have hope? Preposterous. All mythical girls deserve is bottomless despair and death. There's no place for a vessel of evil like you. For the sake of humanity, you should all die."

"What you are saying has no relevance to Ryuunosuke."

"Cling to your dumb hope if you want to—it won't change anything."

"What a pitiful man you are."

Rinne's voice was filled with sadness. She looked at Suberu with pity, as if he was the most miserable creature she'd seen.

"Am I now?"

"I can tell you have never been in love."

"…"

"Had it not been so, you would not harbor the nonsensical wish to destroy the world. Further, you have already proven that your theory about the Sacred Sealing Rings forcing mythical girls to feel attracted to their wearers is incorrect. All I feel for you with your artificial ring is loathing."

Suberu's face became emotionless.

"That's enough," he said impatiently, raising his right hand. "Die. I have already won."

The light of his ring spread out in lines like an electric circuit powering up.

"Ha-ha... It's the world-saving light... Why would he have used this precious light...to aid a devil...?"

Suberu stared at the pulsating light vacantly. In response to his ring, Rinne's Stigma intensified, while the light of her ring weakened.

"Do you know why mythical girls appeared in this world?"

Neither Rinne nor Ranko knew who he was aiming that question at. Maybe at both of them. Or maybe at no one in particular.

Ranko cocked her head.

"Well... There are many theories about that, but no explanation is conclusive. I'm guessing you have it all figured out already, though?"

"You must know why they exist if you want to solve their problem... Find that answer. Unravel the mystery of the purpose of their existence."

For a moment, the briefest of moments, Ranko thought that Suberu's eyes seemed lucid, and he was talking to her in earnestness. But madness overtook him again soon enough.

Suberu spread his arms wide open and yelled, "Awaken, devil! And perish!"

The light of his ring spread farther in circuit-like lines, similar to when Rinne and Ryuunosuke were soul linking, but it went farther than just Suberu's arm, creeping around his whole body.

"Blessed be the wisdom of humanity, which shall triumph over the X factor! I'm the proxy messiah, who will destroy the astral devil hidden in human DNA! I will at last bring peace to humanity, which has foolishly reached a dead end on its path of progress! I will end this passive stopper to our proliferation! Aaah...!"

The light engulfed him.

*   *   *

"Blessed be the spring of my new wooooorrrrrld!"

Suberu's body burst into countless, red particles of light. The traitor's death was shockingly vivid.

"Sara...shina..." Suberu turned out to be an enemy, but Ranko had worked alongside him for a long time. Witnessing his descent into madness and death had to have an emotional effect on her. "What if what he said was not just a madman's gibberish...? No, let us not pursue truth in his insanity."

The traitor had died, but the trouble he'd caused wasn't over. It was only just beginning.

"Ryuunosuke..."

Rinne's ring shattered like a fragile loop of glass, its red light scattering until none was left. Suberu's sacrifice triggered the delinking effect of his synthetic ring, canceling the bond between Ryuunosuke and Rinne.

"Ngh... Aaaaaargh!" Rinne groaned in pain.

The synthetic ring had caused her factor to begin slipping out of her control. Her Valkyrie Dress and weaponry appeared without her wanting them to. Horns, tail, and wings grew out of her body, and her eyes were no longer human, either. Since she was not able to control them, her dragon features manifested as bigger, sharper, or more intense in color.

There was a powerful vibration in the air, like a bass beat. It might have been a pulse of the dragon heart or the quickening before the birth of the devil.

"Ran...ko..."

Rinne's Stigma was spreading over her chest like magma filling fissures in the surface of the earth, glowing ominously in the rhythm of her pulse. Rinne pressed her hands to her chest as if desperately trying to contain the power that was overwhelming her. Her dragon heart was radiating so much heat that it triggered the sprinkler system.

"I feel that...the rage within me is breaking out... Please...tell Ryuunosuke...to never stop...believing in me."

The water from the sprinklers was turning into steam as soon as it hit Rinne's body.

"You must go... I can't...hold it in any longer...!"

"...Okay. I promise, I'll pass your message to Ryuunosuke."

Ranko stood up, clutching her wound, and walked out of the lab room to the hallway.

She coughed.

"Gwah... I'm not in good shape...but I can't die yet."

Having lost a lot of blood, she was deathly pale.

Things could hardly be any worse. The world was threatened with destruction, and she was the only person who knew what was going on. An assassin had been sent to Ryuunosuke, the only person who had a chance of stopping Rinne from going berserk. And Rinne, already at berserk phase one, had to be stopped from progressing to phase two at all costs.

Despite all that, Ranko's lips curved upward in a smile.

"You were so sure you won, Sarashina, but this game's far from over."

This was the least probable, worst-case scenario. But Ranko had prepared for it, too.

"Wait and watch from hell, Sarashina, as your sure victory turns to defeat. There's more than one girl in love with Ryuunosuke."

Love had the power to save the world.

Ranko got a smartphone out of her pocket—one tweaked so that it worked even in the underground facility. She had an idea, rooted in the assumption that Suberu's action until his death followed some logic rather than pure madness. What he'd said earlier might have sounded like gibberish to an ordinary person, but as a mythical girl researcher, Ranko understood it.

"Let's forget about Sarashina for now... Rinne, Dazai boy, don't you die..."

At that moment, the fearsome roar of a dragon shook the research facility to its foundations.

◆

Underground Kokonoe Factor Research Facility, Lab Room Number Five. Heat swirled around the dragon, and when it rose, the dragon roared, announcing with that piercing cry its birth into the human world.

"Heh..."

Rinne's consciousness had faded into the background as the animalistic demon inside her came to the surface. She was no longer Rinne, but a mythical dragon, albeit in human form.

"Ha-ha-ha-ha-ha-ha-ha-ha-ha!"

The dragon's laughter sent vibrations through the building.

"Now, I have no choice but to annihilate this world. Countless humans will die. It would have been better if I had died instead, but why should I when I have done nothing wrong? I will destroy everything. Rather than I, it will be the world that tried to kill me that shall perish."

Its armor, powered by the factor powers, had also become unstable. The right gauntlet kept morphing until it turned into jaws. The dragon raised them, and it lit up with dark-red light. The next moment, it fired a superheated beam, which was incomparably more powerful than the beam Rinne had used against Mari that night in the park two weeks earlier. It shot straight through the entire research facility, built deep underground, all the way to the surface, creating a wide tunnel that glowed red from the heat of the blast. A hot air current flew upward from the hellishly hot lab room where the dragon was.

"I can see the sky."

The dragon gazed up through the tunnel and stood still. Was it because its body hadn't yet adapted to the second phase of berserk status, or because it was moved by the sight of the sky, which it had never seen before...?

After some time had passed, the dragon in human form unfurled its wings and allowed the air current to lift it. The sky at the end of the tunnel grew bigger and bigger, until the dragon was soaring in it. The sky was a mix of red and black, the red more intense than the colors of the setting sun, and the black darker than the darkest hour of the night. It was an exceedingly rare phenomenon caused by a mythical girl descending into berserk phase two.

The dragon looked down at the ground. It could see the sprawling research facility and the hills, and in the distance—a city, where people were going about their daily lives without any idea about the approaching apocalypse.

The dragon aimed the jaw-gauntlet at the city without showing any emotion.

"Let's set off some fireworks to cheer up my pitiful former self."

The dragon readied to fire a beam powerful enough to burn the whole world to the ground. The smoldering evil within it would not subside until everything had been eaten up by the flames of its rage.

But it did not fire that beam.

"Take that!"

A golden-haired girl dressed in red suddenly attacked the dragon, which had to raise its jaw-gauntlet to block the girl's weapon. A metallic sound reverberated around them as their weapons collided. The girl had used the momentum of her attack to push the dragon to the ground.

"Tsk! A pesky fly."

The dragon glared as the golden-haired girl in a beautiful crimson dress slowly descended from the sky, smiling fearlessly.

"Whoa, look at you! You're a mess. It really doesn't suit you."

The girl didn't have a Stigma on her chest. On her ring finger was a hallowed ring. She was the Fifth Factor girl, a vampire.

And she wasn't alone.

"Rinne!"

The vampire girl set down the boy she'd been carrying.

"We've come to save you!" the boy said, facing the dragon.

The vampire called him.

"Ryuunosuke!"

She embraced him from behind.

"Do it, Marie," he replied.

The way they addressed each other had changed, indicating that they were now closer than before.

The vampire girl opened her mouth wide and bit the boy's neck.

"Nnh…"

He shuddered, experiencing not pain but mind-blowing pleasure in his entire body. The vampire shot the dragon a provocative look while sucking the boy's blood, placing her left hand on Ryuunosuke's chest to show off her ring.

The dragon watched this suggestive display without moving an inch. The vampire knew that, even in berserk status, the dragon wouldn't interfere until she had finished her meal, understanding that it was the vampire's declaration of war.

The vampire withdrew her fangs, briefly remaining connected to the boy by a thread of her saliva mixed with his blood.

"This is what real bloodsucking is like. Are you jealous, dragon?"

The vampire licked her mouth clean.

"Ryuunosuke has wed me, and I've drunk real blood. I've never felt stronger in my life!"

She laughed and conjured an enormous blood weapon.

"The dragon hunt begins!"

The vampire and her boy engaged the dragon in a battle to save the world.

CHAPTER 5

Cataclysmal Ragnarok

A little earlier, before the vampire and dragon's battle…

The assassin fired his gun, and the bullet flew toward Ryuunosuke Dazai, its momentum making the air friction and gravity inconsequential. Ryuunosuke had nothing to shield himself from the bullet, and at that range, he couldn't dodge it, either. It would take a mere fraction of a second for the deadly piece of lead to hit him.

"It's over…"

But the bullet never reached him. The extreme situation flooded Ryuunosuke's brain with adrenaline, which sharpened his senses and made everything seem to move in slow motion. He saw every detail of the person who flew in among shards of broken glass and wood; she was a beautiful golden-haired girl with spellbinding eyes framed by long eyelashes.

Then the flow of time returned to normal. She shouldn't have been there, yet she was, and she'd just saved his life.

"Abara…?"

Mari Vlad Abara, dressed in her school uniform, had burst through the window to shield Ryuunosuke from the bullet with her own body.

"Ow, you grazed my hand."

She opened her fist, and the bullet tumbled to the floor.

"You...caught the bullet with your bare hand...?" Kuroi asked with shocked dread.

"What's so surprising about that?"

"You're a monster...!"

"Yeah. So what?"

Kuroi fired several shots at her in succession. She flicked each bullet away with just one hand. Guns didn't work on mythical girls. Neither Rinne nor Mari would suffer meaningful damage from rapid gunfire. Even if the shooter managed to hit an important organ, the mythical girl would only suffer from a temporary decrease in her abilities while she quickly regenerated.

"Die!"

Mari attacked, instantly closing the distance to Kuroi. Her swift steps ripped the tatami mats off the floor. She kicked the man in the stomach.

"Bwargh!"

She literally sent him flying out of the living room, through the hallway, and out the front door until he crashed into the garden wall opposite the house, smashing it. There he lay, motionless.

Ryuunosuke had been watching in shocked bewilderment.

"Is... Is he dead?"

"Dunno. I tried to be gentle."

"You told him to die!"

"Did I?" she asked indifferently.

"Sorry. I should've thanked you first."

"I helped you because I wanted to. You don't need a reason to help people. Isn't that right?" she repeated what he'd once told her.

What goes around, comes around.

"Abara..."

"It's my first time visiting your house, and I'd love to just chill, but let's get away from here for now. People will come nosing around, attracted by the noise, and I don't think either of us wants to deal with them."

"Yeah, okay. But there was another guy, Mr. Yanagida..."

"The big man in a suit? He's fine. Tough for a human. The bullets didn't pass through anything major, so don't worry about leaving him for a bit; he won't die."

"Oh, if you say so…"

Ryuunosuke decided to trust her judgment. He got out his phone and called for an ambulance, describing the emergency with as little detail as he could get away with. Once that was done, he grabbed his shoes from the entrance hall, and he and Mari left through the window in Ranko's room. The back of his house faced the woods. If they walked for a short while through them, they'd reach a small, rarely visited park. He went there with Mari, and the two of them sat on benches in an gazebo at the center of the park.

"Oof…"

Ryuunosuke breathed deeply with relief, feeling the tension leave his body.

The sun was beginning to set. The lamps on the eastern side of the park were already turning on.

"I thought I was going to die, for real."

"There was no danger of that. I've been keeping watch over you."

"No way! Since when?!"

"Since you were taken home without the dragon girl."

"Really, you've been following us the whole time? I know I should be thankful you saved me at all, but why did you have to wait until the last minute? I almost pissed my pants."

"Sorry, but I couldn't reveal myself too early and alert that thug. Besides, I wasn't sure what was going to happen. Saving you at the last minute made me look even cooler, no?"

"I'd have thought so, if it weren't for the fact that you deliberately waited until I almost got shot! But why were you keeping watch over me anyway?"

"Ranko asked me to."

Ryuunosuke wasn't expecting Ranko's name to come up.

"We met up one night about two weeks ago. Bold of her to trust me… But then again, I'm too nice to people sometimes."

"You met up with President two weeks ago…?"

That rang a bell. Ryuunosuke remembered Ranko going out on the first night of the Dragon Babysitter Project.

"She asked me to meet her at Chandelier near the station to talk about you. I considered it might've been a trap, but if she gave me any trouble, I'd just slaughter everyone, no problem. I was curious what she wanted, so I went."

Ryuunosuke couldn't hide his astonishment at Ranko's secret schemes.

"She turned up alone; can you believe it? Without a single body-guard. She'd stand no chance against me. I thought she was being stupid, but it also convinced me her request was personal."

"So anyway, what did you talk about?"

"This and that, nothing too important. Mostly about you."

"…? About me?"

"Ranko said that if I got removed from my mission, you might be in danger. 'What makes you say I'd lose my job?' I asked her. 'My general analysis of the situation from various perspectives. Best to play it safe,' she said. I told her, 'So it's just your hunch, is it?!' Honestly, I don't know what she's thinking, that Ranko. But even though she's my enemy, on a personal level, I trust her."

Mari was tracing a circle on the ground with the tip of her loafer.

"And then it happened, just like she said. I got reassigned. That spooked me into thinking you might get killed, so I kept watch over you."

"Okay, I get the picture… But why would anyone want to kill me? My ring would have some value to your organization; I get that, but why kill me?"

"It wasn't the Order trying to kill you. I believe Loki was acting on his own initiative."

"Who or what is that?"

"The Order's spy at the Calamity Research Institute. He goes by the name *Sarashina* there, I think."

"What?! Mr. Sarashina is a spy...?! Wait, should you be telling me this? Aren't you going to get in trouble for colluding with the enemy?"

"I don't care anymore. I've had enough of being the Order's pawn or Loki's pawn. Loki used to be my superior. I have no idea what he's planning, but it doesn't seem to have anything to do with the Order's policies."

In the eyes of Ranko Akeda, a Calamity Research Institute researcher, Ryuunosuke's murder would be the worst-case scenario. Having him kidnapped by the Order in the case of him and Rinne getting split up wasn't what she was worried about. Sure, it would be a significant loss to the CRI, but it would be of no consequence to the world as long as Ryuunosuke remained alive. Ranko knew the Order wouldn't kill him. They might keep him in captivity and experiment on him, but not kill him.

Suppose, though, that there was traitor who had their own plans, contradictory to the Order's, and killing Ryuunosuke was a part of them. Mari would be an inconvenience to this traitor. Ranko had warned Mari about this, just in case her worst fears turned out to be true. She told the vampire girl that if she suddenly got removed from her mission, it would mean someone might try to kill Ryuunosuke.

"I didn't quite believe it at first. The man who tried to shoot you wasn't working for the Order, by the way. Loki must have recruited him from the CRI."

Ryuunosuke's phone began ringing.

"It's President!"

"Answer," Mari hurried him.

Ryuunosuke put the phone to his ear.

"Hello?! President, where are you?!"

"You're alive. Good. I'm at the facility."

There was a lot of noise on the line, and Ryuunosuke could hear a loud alarm in the background. There was clearly an emergency at the research facility. Ranko's voice sounded weak, without its usual smugness.

There was supposed to be no way to contact anyone at the facility, but Ranko must have set up some emergency phone access.

"President… Are you okay?"

"Yes, I'm fine. You?"

"Kuroi tried to kill me, but Abara saved me."

"Good, I knew she'd come to your rescue. So Kuroi was the spy in Section One… Would be good if he was still alive… Well, it's no longer checkmate. Luck's on our side."

"What 'checkmate'…?"

"No matter. Listen, Dazai boy," Ranko said with urgency.

"Yes…?"

"In brief, Sarashina betrayed us. Rinne has been unlinked from you."

"What?! H-how?!"

"Sarashina created a synthetic ring. He's dead now, but he triggered Rinne's berserk phase two. She's a walking time bomb. If we don't stop her, she'll destroy the world."

"Rinne's gone berserk…?!"

"The situation—" Ranko was interrupted by a fit of coughing.

"What's wrong?"

"Don't mind me. The situation is as bad as you can imagine. We don't have much time left, and our chances of stopping Rinne are low. You would be risking your life—"

"If you need me to do the saving, I will," Ryuunosuke interrupted, without making it clear whether he meant saving the world, Rinne, or both.

There was no hint of hesitation in his voice.

"You're the man."

"I try to be."

"I wish I could see you now. Should've made it a video call. So Rinne is at berserk phase two, but please don't give up on her. You must believe in her."

"Of course. Where is she?"

"In the underground lab, but not for long—"

The call abruptly ended, and at the same time, there was an explosion to the west of where Ryuunosuke and Mari were. Ryuunosuke turned in that direction and saw a beam of light shoot upward from the ground and pierce the clouds. The dark-red light spread through the sky like ink in water.

It didn't look like a natural phenomenon. Awe-inspiring and beautiful, yet sinister and supernatural. It made Ryuunosuke gasp.

"A dark crimson twilight… It's the Ragnarok phenomenon, caused by the second stage of a mythical girl going berserk…," Mari muttered, staring up at the sky blankly. "It means the dragon girl doesn't have much time left…"

Mythical girls would lose their sanity at berserk phase two. Ryuunosuke declared he'd save the world, or Rinne, or both, but he didn't really have a plan. It was up to him to do something, that much was certain, but alone, he couldn't hope to stop the berserk Rinne.

The answer to his dilemma was right in front of him.

"Abara…"

"Right, right. I heard everything—my hearing's pretty sharp. So let me guess, you want me to help you save the girl, and the world while we're at it?"

"Um, yeah."

"Preventing a class-one cataclysm is part of my duties, and I'm not against teaming up with you for that cause. And since it's you asking, I'd be happy to help…"

"So let's do thi—"

Mari silenced him, pressing a finger to his lips.

"That's what I should do as the Order's Ritter, but I have my personal opinion. I don't like volunteering to do extra work, and I don't want to take you somewhere you will most likely die, either. I don't want you to die, Ryuunosuke Dazai."

She knelt on the ground and looked up into his eyes, holding his hands.

"I have a better idea. Will you please listen?" she said.

Ryuunosuke held the gaze of her beautiful eyes.

"Why don't we run away together?" the vampire proposed. "Forget about trying to save the world—that's just stupid. Let's drop it all and escape somewhere we can enjoy our last moments together. I don't mind dying if I get to be together with you. Thinking about it now, the only way I want to die is with you."

"Abara..."

"Don't try to save her—it's impossible. She's already gone berserk; no one can stop her from self-destructing. She's lost her sanity, turning into a beast. She's unable to consent to soul linking, so you can't link with her. It's a checkmate situation, no matter what Ranko said on the phone. Don't go—you can't save anyone, and you'll just end up getting killed."

Ryuunosuke thought that Mari didn't sound as confident as usual. At that moment, she wasn't a mythical vampire girl; she was just a regular girl, a high schooler one year his junior.

"Look at the sky," she said.

Ryuunosuke did as she asked. The dark-red sky really looked apocalyptic.

"It's the end of the world. It's unique scenery caused by a mythical girl. We are monsters who should never have been born, who everyone wants dead. But I'm asking you as a human..."

Under that ominous sky, the girl pleaded with the boy with all her heart.

"...let's run away as far as we can. It might be too late, and we might die while running, but it's still better that way. It's a choice you can make. It might be a bad choice to make, running away when the world is ending, and some people may blame us, but so what? This world isn't worth saving anyway. Sooner or later, I'd be executed, or I'd go berserk and self-destruct. I have only one wish... Let's throw it all to hell and enjoy each other," she tempted.

Ryuunosuke imagined spending the last days, or minutes maybe, of the dying world with Mari. Letting go of all obligations and feigning ignorance as everything died—Rinne and the world. Mari might be right about the chances of saving the world at that stage being zero. If it was too late anyway, they might as well make a run for it, and nobody would point a finger at them. He could accept the end of the world as a fact instead of struggling in vain. It was an option. It certainly was...

"Sorry, Abara."

...but it wasn't an option Ryuunosuke would ever consider. Mari must have known this.

"I can't. I don't care if I die. Not to say I want to die...but I can't leave Rinne like that and run away. I don't know if it's possible to save her or not; maybe it's not, like you say, but it's impossible for me to just give up on her. You understand this about me, no?"

"..."

Ryuunosuke stood from the bench and looked Mari in the eyes.

"You said you don't want me to die, so help me. Let's do this together and survive. You don't seem to value your own life, but I do. I want you to live on. If you care about me, then live, fight to stay alive, and if it turns out to be no use, then we'll die together. Can you do that for me, Marie?"

He called her by her preferred name to show that he was sincere. He was entirely reliant on her help, so he tried everything to get her on board.

"...Tee-hee."

Mari's giggle conveyed a mixture of emotions: resignation, sadness, envy, joy, respect, pessimism, yearning, and a tiny bit of jealousy. She didn't tell him, "It's because you're like this that you stole my heart," biting her tongue before the words were out.

"I was only joking earlier. You know that, right? If you said yes, I'd have punched you right in the face!"

She stood up, still holding his hands. And on one of his hands was the ray of hope. She'd do anything for him.

"Okay, let's save that idiot, and the world while we're at it!"

"Thanks, Marie!"

Mari nodded.

"Ryuunosuke…"

She let go of his hands and took one step back. Her face flushed red.

"Before we go, though…I…I have a request…"

"What is it this time?"

Mari fidgeted, suddenly acting coy.

"Would you…w-wed me, too?" she asked, looking up at him with a pout as if she was upset that she had to ask.

"It—it doesn't mean anything special to me; there's no deeper meaning to it, obviously, but I just thought it might help us in the upcoming battle. It's just to boost my factor powers, giving us slightly better odds of saving that reptilian dumbass. I don't particularly care either way, but it would give us an edge… No, you know what, forget I asked. No need to wed…um, soul link with me—we'll be fine without it, I'm sure," Mari said hurriedly, embarrassed.

"No, let's do it."

"Huh…? You're really casual about this, aren't you?"

Mari looked at Ryuunosuke with dissatisfaction.

"Casual? I just think it's a good idea. It's going to make you stronger, right? I've been thinking for some time that I should link with you, and I really wish now I'd done it earlier. I was told to hold off on it, but we've got an emergency on our hands."

"Argh, you! How can you be so insensitive, you jerk?!"

"What…? Do you not want to link with me after all?"

"I do!!!"

Mari turned her face away from him and began to unfasten the buttons of her uniform shirt. She had to do that to give him access to the Stigma on her chest, of course, so her intentions weren't inappropriate. But still, Ryuunosuke got nervous and didn't know where to look.

Mari opened up the top of her shirt. Her bra was showing. Ryuunosuke wasn't making any move toward Mari, staying rooted to the spot as the poor girl waited.

"So, um... Are you sure this is going to work without you being even a little bit berserk?"

"What? Oh, I...don't know... We'll just have to try..."

"It really is a shotgun soul wedding. Neither of us came prepared," Ryuunosuke joked, and they both laughed, their moods lifting.

Mari's Stigma appeared on her chest, and simultaneously, Ryuunosuke's ring lit up. It was generating heat, expanding and spreading over his entire arm.

"Ryuunosuke," Mari said resolutely, but with affection. "Touch me."

He nodded and reached toward her chest. His fingers touched the mark.

"In sickness and in health, in joy and in sorrow, for richer and for poorer..." She began reciting the pledge in a clear, sonorous voice. "...do you vow to stand behind me, to be my support, my companion..."

She knew the sacred formula for binding souls together.

"...to be mine from now until the world ends?"

"I do."

As she spoke, the light of her Stigma faded, while the light of Ryuunosuke's ring burst into glittering speckles that surrounded both of them. The speckles were floating toward Mari's mark, as if it was pulling them toward it.

"Nngh!"

Mari fidgeted. Her Stigma disappeared, and a ring of light formed around her ring finger. A tiara woven of light briefly appeared on her head before dispersing into darkness.

Their soul linking was complete.

Mari traced her new ring with the index finger of her right hand. She lifted her hand to gaze elatedly at this symbol of her bond with Ryuunosuke.

"...You put a ring on my finger, Ryuunosuke."

She giggled.

"Huh? Ah, yep."

"Not the least excited, are you?"

"Well, it's my second time around."

"Urgh, you!"

Mari face-palmed, but then she extended her hand to Ryuunosuke.

"Okay, let's fly right over to that idiot. Can't keep her waiting forever."

"Sure."

Ryuunosuke took Mari's hand in his.

"Oh, by the way, there's something I want to do in front of her."

"Yeah? What is it?"

A mischievous but still beautiful smile appeared on Mari's lips.

"Can't you guess? Let me suck you right in front of her."

◆

Back to the present moment.

After some bloodsucking, Mari the vampire was ready to battle the dragon.

The vampire landed on the asphalt parking lot of the research facility in the middle of a forest. She set down Ryuunosuke behind her and turned toward the dragon. The sky above them was an apocalyptic mix of red and black.

Mari wasn't going to kill the dragon, nor beat her in battle, nor capture her. She was going to save her.

"Marie," Ryuunosuke called.

"Yes?"

"You can do this."

"Sure. Don't move an inch and leave it all to me!"

She sensed him nodding his head behind her.

Mari remembered something Rinne had said to her.

"You are strong…but I have Ryuunosuke."

She could understand now exactly how Rinne had felt back then. It wasn't just that the soul linking had made her stronger. Having Ryuunosuke standing behind her, cheering her on, gave her so much confidence, she believed there was no way she'd lose.

"Why did you bother to come here, vampire? The world's annihilation cannot be stopped," the dragon said.

"Everything in the world belongs to me. Don't you dare destroy it. And you're a part of my world, too, so I'm not losing you, either, you dumb dragon... Ugh, I don't think any of what I'm saying is getting to her."

The body of Rinne Irako housed a very different entity. Having gone berserk, Rinne's inner devil came to the surface, while her own consciousness had faded somewhere deep. There was no telling if she had any awareness of what was going on, but Mari kept trying to talk to her despite that.

"Looks like I'll just have to save you."

Mari was going to stick with Ryuunosuke's reckless plan until the end. It might be suicide—a suicide in which the world would die with her. Not a bad way to go out. She'd assumed her life would end like this anyway.

"Your conceit is laughable, vampire." The dragon made a move. "You, saving me? What nonsense."

It lifted its right gauntlet, which had become so enormous that it was dragging on the ground, then aimed it, ready to fire...

"Ryuunosuke?!"

Mari swung her polearm and blocked the dragon's attack with the ax edge. The ground shook from the thunderous impact.

Without a shadow of doubt, the dragon's target had been Ryuunosuke.

"Rinne..."

Ryuunosuke had not moved from his spot even as the shock wave of the dragon's attack hit him. He was only spectating.

"There can be no salvation for the world, which defined us as destroyers who need be excised. A world that branded you a sinner for merely existing deserves to be annihilated. That is only logical, is it not?" the dragon asked.

"You're not Rinne anymore. She'd never raise her hand at Ryuunosuke."

Mari had no doubt that her rival Rinne loved Ryuunosuke as much as she did. She needed no further proof that the creature in front of her wasn't Rinne.

"If you're not her, I definitely won't let you lay a finger on Ryuunosuke!"

If the dragon was targeting Ryuunosuke, Mari had to move it safely away from him. Ryuunosuke was both central to the battle strategy and to Mari. Yet she couldn't put too much distance between herself and the boy, or the soul linking effects would weaken.

Mari decided to take this battle...to the sky.

"Raaargh!"

Mari spun her polearm around and picked up Rinne with the butt end.

"So heavy...!"

The density of Rinne's body broke the laws of physics. Mari's joints cracked under the weight.

"Hup!"

Mari kicked the halberd scythe, bouncing the dragon upward. She then stuck the pointy end of the weapon into the ground and vaulted at the dragon, kicking it skyward.

The dragon didn't resist this. Once in the air, it simply opened its wings.

"Got you where I want you!"

Mari grew one wing, then another, and another, until she had four. She spread them out and flew in pursuit of the dragon. Her flying capabilities were enhanced by the soul linking and having had real blood. Without the ring's boost, she wouldn't have been able to fly with Ryuunosuke all the way from the park near his house.

Mari overtook the dragon, but as soon as she was ahead of it, it pointed a gauntlet at her. The transformed piece of armor was in turret mode, glowing from the inside ominously. Mari knew the name of that weapon.

"Fafnir?!"

A black beam of dragon breath shot into the sky, piercing the clouds.

"You gave me a scare there, but at least you can't pull that off again for a while..."

As she was saying that, the dragon lined up with her, aiming the jaw-turret at her once more. Mari saw energy gathering inside it again.

"You can't shoot it again so soon after the first one, right?"

The darkness within the turret rapidly intensified.

"Seriously?!"

"Rrrrrraaaaaaaaaarrrgh!"

The dragon unleashed another beam attack, roaring. This time, it grazed one of Mari's wings, which burned to ash. Mari was fine, though. The beam shot past her, hitting a mountain in the distance.

"Whoa..."

There was a flash of light, followed by a shock wave and the loud *boom* of a terrifying explosion as half of the mountain was blasted away, the trees on the remaining, smoldering part of it flattened. There was a tremor like an earthquake. The shock wave knocked back Mari slightly.

"How can you have this much firepower...?"

In berserk state, the dragon heart generated limitless amounts of heat.

The dragon wasn't finished attacking. It raised its gauntlet, pointing it at the sky.

"Another shot? No..."

Having fought Rinne before, Mari recognized the switch from Fafnir to Gram. The dragon used the remnant heat from the last shot to transform the gauntlet into a sword no less than a hundred meters long. It swung that ridiculously long sword downward.

Mari dodged to the side and saw the dark beam scorch the ground barely meters away from Ryuunosuke.

"Ryuunosuke...!"

"I'm fine!" he shouted back from the ground.

Ryuunosuke hadn't moved from his spot. He was watching the aerial battle without fear or worry in his eyes, but on closer inspection, his fists were clenched so tight, his fingernails were digging into his skin, making it bleed.

He'd asked Mari for help and entrusted the fighting to her, but that left him feeling pitifully powerless. What he was fighting with were his emotions.

After multiple beam shots, the dragon's gauntlet finally stopped glowing, going into cooldown mode. Still...

"You're too overpowered!" Mari grumbled.

The dragon had excellent flying ability and attacks with insane range. When Rinne wasn't berserk, she could shoot beams powered by the heat of her dragon heart, but not in close succession since the shots cooled her back down and she needed time to charge them, too. In berserk mode, though, the dragon heart was a source of infinite heat, making rapid, consecutive beam attacks possible. Even immediately after the shots, there was plenty of leftover heat to utilize in battle.

Then there was the matter of the destructive power of the dragon's attacks. If one shot could blow away a mountain, Mari had to do everything and anything to prevent the dragon from firing down at the ground, or Ryuunosuke would be done for. This meant that Mari had to keep her position above the dragon, even though she wasn't as good a flier. She wasn't as strong, either. In this battle, she was without question at a considerable disadvantage.

"Whatever. I'm not going to cry about this being unfair."

Mari told Ryuunosuke he could leave this to her, and she wouldn't disappoint him. She kept her promises.

When a mythical girl went berserk, there were three main phases. At phase one, she lost the ability to deactivate her factor powers and physical features.

At phase two—which Rinne was at—she lost her powers of reason. Her own consciousness would fade while her inner devil took over.

At phase three, the final stage, the mythical girl would become a force of destruction. The damage she would be capable of depended on her factor. In the dragon factor's case, what happened was very simple— the dragon heart would enter a critical state and cause a massive explosion. This had to be prevented at all costs.

"I'll stop you before it gets to that, I swear."

Mari lunged at the dragon, swinging down with her halberd scythe.

The blade sliced deep into the dragon's gauntlet, breaking its heat-discharge functionality. This hindered the Gram and Fafnir attacks, at least temporarily. Being so close to the dragon, Mari was getting burned by the heat emanating from it, but her skin kept regenerating. She didn't show her pain, attacking repeatedly until she and the dragon became locked together, spiraling down to the ground. Just before hitting it, they sprang away from each other, landing a short distance apart.

"Surrender, vampire. Like me, you must desire the end of this world. Allow me to deliver it."

"I want many things, but the apocalypse isn't one of them."

"You and I are of the same kind. How can we disagree? If the world wants us dead, we must kill it. It is a basic self-preservation instinct."

"Thanks for the lecture. Do all the devils inside mythical girls have a last-boss spiel like that? Anyway, why were you trying to kill Ryuunosuke?"

"I wished to free myself from my shackles."

"Shackles? What?"

"His existence shackles 'me.' He binds me, through the lingering love 'I' feel for him. As long as he lives, 'I' cannot give in to the lust for destruction, but I must destroy the world for 'my' sake. That is why I must... I must kill him first..."

"Your eyes..."

The dragon's eyes were brimming with tears. The heat of the dragon's fury was evaporating them before they spilled out.

"What is this? Tears?"

Surprised, the dragon wiped its already dry eyes.

I get it, thought Mari. *I get it, as another mythical girl. We curse the world, we curse our fate, and we wish we'd never been born. We grow up hating ourselves. But he—he isn't like that.*

"Ryuunosuke is our polar opposite. That's what made us fall in love with him...," she said, partly to Rinne, partly to herself.

Ryuunosuke was steadfast in his desire to help everyone. The mythical girls were his opposite. It was this extreme difference that attracted them to him.

The dragon and the vampire got along like a cat and dog, but they had their love for Ryuunosuke in common. When it came to him, they understood each other.

"Listen, Rinne," Mari said, stressing her rival's name.

Understanding Rinne's feelings only made her annoyed.

"You hate this world, but this is the world he lives in," she said sharply, trying to get her point across.

Mari completely understood what Rinne was feeling, and that's why she could be sure what Rinne was doing was wrong.

"Now, you idiot, prove you're worthy to see your crush again!"

Mari dissolved her Bloody Maiden weapon and jumped far back. She was preparing for the final showdown. This hopeless idiot had to be saved from herself, but it wasn't Mari's job to do that. She'd only set the stage. She wanted to accomplish the setup perfectly.

"Nosferatu, full release!"

At her command, the limiters on her Valkyrie Dress's enhanced Reginleif blood weapon, Nosferatu, became disabled.

Factor abilities couldn't be used constantly—utilize them too aggressively, and you'd run out of factor power, rendering you unable to fight. Removing the limiters on your factor greatly increased your strength at the cost of skyrocketing your power consumption. A mythical girl couldn't fight very long in their unrestrained state, so it was a last resort tactic.

Mari wouldn't have much time left before she depleted her energy, but then again, Rinne's time was running out, too. Mari had to settle this quickly.

Suddenly, there were blades all around the dragon.

"?!"

Crimson weapons—scythes, swords, axes, guillotines—floated in the air around it. The dragon was taken by surprise, trapped in a cage of blades. This was...

"Gungnir, the Torture Chamber!"

The blood weapons began to rotate, swishing through the air. Each of them capable of slicing through an armored tank, they flew at the dragon all at once, spinning at a thousand rotations per minute.

Mari's plan was simple. As long as the dragon's head was still attached to its torso, it would be able to recover using the dragon-factor regeneration ability. So Mari was going to slice off the dragon's limbs with her master move.

Centrifugal force broke the weapons into pieces. They turned into blood fog that was too thick to see what had been left of her opponent.

When it came to overall battle ability, the vampire factor was top-rated, and Mari Vlad Abara was the strongest vampire mythical girl known to history. Not only did she possess a natural talent, but she'd also undergone spartan training to bring out the most of her abilities. She never doubted her strength.

Mari had this to say about the dragon factor.

"You're a monster...!"

The dragon emerged from the blood fog.

"Are you finished?"

Its wings were in tatters, but it had no noticeable wounds on its body. It must have wrapped itself in its wings for cover, sacrificing the ability to fly to prevent significant damage.

"How freaking tough are you to resist that slaughterfest?!"

Mari's master move had failed. Her shoulders slumped, and she sighed. After that attack, without any limiters on her powers, she didn't have much juice left. She was out of options...

"I really didn't want to do this..."

Could Mari have it in her to pull off another attack?

She extended her arm in front of her, spreading her fingers open with her palm facing upward. She had one last ace up her sleeve, and she was going to use the very remainder of her power for it.

"Bloody Mary!"

Mari snapped her hand shut. Nothing happened. No bloody stakes appeared, no blades, nothing. But it would be a mistake to assume Mari's skill had not taken effect.

"Bwah!" The dragon suddenly covered its mouth, coughing up blood. "What…is this…?"

It stared at its bloodied hand in confusion.

"Don't know what I did to you, huh?"

Having used two special moves without limiters, Mari ran out of power. Her Valkyrie Dress disappeared with no energy to sustain it. Mari was back in her school uniform.

She had already won when she used Gungnir. Bloody Mary was its secondary effect, which could only be activated when factor limiters were disabled. When the Gungnir weapons dissolved, Bloody Mary morphed the copious blood mist breathed in by the target into sharp awls, which elongated, piercing the target's organs.

"You're tough on the outside, but vulnerable on the inside. This line of attack was so easy to figure out, but not for an all-brawn-no-brain devil, I guess. Rinne wouldn't have fallen for it, breathing in the blood mist."

Mari was on her last legs, her eyes unfocused, but she smiled victoriously. She'd known from the start that even if her Gungnir failed to deal any external damage, the dragon would be unable to defend itself from internal damage.

The dragon stopped moving. Then it dropped to the ground, falling to one knee.

"This body…will not obey me…?" it said, stupefied.

Mari had targeted the dragon heart. It would explode only when triggered by internal processes, not from taking direct physical damage. The vampire reckoned that injuring the dragon's most important organ would result in all its energy being directed to regenerating it, temporarily incapacitating the dragon. And it'd gone according to plan.

"Over to you…Ryuunosuke…"

"I got this."

Mari slumped onto the ground, falling unconscious after exhausting her factor powers and pushing herself past her limits.

"My turn!"

Ryuunosuke broke into a run.

◆

At last, the waiting was over. It was his turn to jump into action. That was all the boy was thinking about.

Not for a moment did he fear Mari would lose or make a deadly mistake. She told him to leave the battle to her, and he fully trusted in her capability.

Finally, his turn had come.

Being able to only watch as Mari fought had been agonizing for him. Ashamed of his powerlessness, he'd been grinding his teeth until one cracked.

"Rinne!" he called to the kneeling, motionless dragon, which was surrounded by heat haze.

Hot air currents were pushing Ryuunosuke away. As he got close, his skin began to burn.

Mari was fighting in this furnace?! But I have to keep going to reach Rinne...

Ignoring the heat as best he could, Ryuunosuke pushed on to get closer to Rinne. Every time he got nearer, his eyes would dry up, and his skin would burn. His body would auto-regenerate, though, thanks to him sharing the vampire factor's restorative ability through his soul link with Mari.

His plan was simple—touch Rinne's Stigma to soul link with her and end her berserk status. He focused his eyes on the mark. He was almost there. Just a little farther...

Ryuunosuke's ring activated, and light enveloped his left arm. He reached toward the Stigma, which was glowing red.

"Aaaaaaarrrrrgh! It burrrrrnnnnsss!"

That heat was too much even for the vampire factor's auto-regen. Ryuunosuke's skin blistered, exposing the flesh underneath, which was scorched all the way to the bone, and searing his nerves. All that was left of his left arm was its outline, made of light created by the Sacred Sealing Ring, which kept glowing just as brightly as before.

The pain was driving Ryuunosuke crazy, the deadly heat making his self-preservation instinct scream to run away. But if he did run away, it would be all over. He had to suppress this desperate urge to escape, withstand the pain and the heat. It hurt so much, Ryuunosuke felt like he was going to pass out, but then the same pain brought him back to his senses. It was torture for his brain.

"Gaaaaaaaaaaaaaaah!"

Ryuunosuke couldn't help screaming. He could only bottle up his suffering for so long.

He kept trying to reach for the Stigma but couldn't. It was as if there was an invisible wall between him and Rinne, shutting him out. She was so close to him, yet so far.

Even as the pain from his burned right arm was threatening to drive him insane, Ryuunosuke sensed that the heat coming from Rinne was fueled by rage which had long lain dormant, by her anger at the world, by her indignation at the injustice she'd met with.

"Do not touch me…! I will… I will kill you! I will not let you…do this to me…!" Rinne's devil shrieked.

Ryuunosuke, with his ring, which could suppress the evil entities within mythical girls, was the devil's archenemy. On top of that, Rinne's devil saw him as a shackle preventing it from running rampant—he had to be killed.

"What idiot would stop at this point?! There's no going back!" Ryuunosuke yelled back.

"A world that brands one a sinner for merely having been born, denying them the right to live and sentencing them to death, is devoid of meaning! Do you deny it?! I have not done anything to deserve this death sentence, and so I shall condemn this rotten world to death instead! I am doing this for you, too! I love you with all my heart! Why can you not see it? Why do you reject my love?!"

"What sort of twisted logic is that?! It's making my brain hurt! You don't even know what life is about, edgelord! You're not Rinne! She'd never give me this dumb doom talk!"

"If you care about 'me,' then die! That is all I am asking! That is all I want! How do I make you understand? I love you! So please die for me! I wish to give you the sweetest of deaths!"

"You're making zero sense! If you love someone, you don't want to freaking kill them! Do you have any brain at all?!"

The dragon was radiating such ferocious heat...

"I will have you answer one question."

...yet its voice was chillingly cold.

"The question I asked you that night. You pretended not to hear."

Ryuunosuke shuddered, forgetting all about his pain.

"..."

He knew exactly what night she was talking about. He remembered her asking him a question as he felt her warmth against his back. He didn't answer her then, not wanting to hurt her feelings. He didn't want to tell her what he really thought, nor lie to her. He chose the third option, which was to pretend he didn't hear her.

"Do you think some people do not deserve to live?"

Just being a mythical girl was a death sentence. Every day brought Rinne closer to her execution. Knowing that, Ryuunosuke hadn't been ready to answer her that night. He'd pretended not to hear, but she'd seen through his weakness.

"Do you think some people do not deserve to live?" The dragon repeated Rinne's question.

"I think..."

That everyone deserves to live. All humans are equal, and their lives have equal value, equal importance. We should accept everyone, as fellow members of Mothership Earth.

Of course not!

It wasn't the world Ryuunosuke was trying to save. It was Rinne. It just so happened that saving her would save the world as well. And he couldn't save her by telling her he thought nobody deserved to be killed. He had to shake her to reach her.

Ryuunosuke took in a deep breath, the hot air burning his lungs, his mouth dry as parchment, and shouted the reply he'd been too scared to give her that night.

"Some people deserve to die!"

That was his honest opinion, which he'd normally keep to himself. He'd finally made up his mind to tell Rinne the truth rather than a pretty little lie that might make him sound like more of a bighearted person than he really was.

He'd sensed the agonizing heat coming from the dragon was an expression of long-suppressed anger and despair that Rinne had to endure this whole time. He wanted to save her from that world of pain.

"I believe there are people who deserve to die! People this world would be better off without! It's sad, but some people are beyond redemption!"

Not every life was equal. Not every person was equal. Their value varied from one to another.

"The value, the importance of a life depends on a person! Everyone thinks that; they just don't say it out loud! They don't want to come off as cruel, so they pretend to value everyone the same, spouting the same Goody Two-shoes nonsense so that nobody would point a finger at them! But everyone understands this game! There are lots of people nobody cares about, because most people care only about themselves! They don't care if others live or die!"

Mythical girls, who had the power to destroy the world, certainly didn't have many people's sympathy.

"But you know what, Rinne?!"

This was what he'd wanted her to hear the most.

"You're not one of the people who deserve to die! At least, that's what I think!"

He noticed the dragon's petite shoulders twitch.

Ryuunosuke wasn't used to shouting, and his voice was breaking. It didn't help that his throat had been so dried by the hot air, its membranes were breaking, leaking blood. But he had to keep talking to Rinne. She might be the gravest danger the world had ever known, but she'd become someone who mattered a lot to Ryuunosuke. The soul linking ritual wouldn't work without the consent of both parties. Rinne had gone berserk, and her consciousness was locked somewhere deep, so she couldn't give her consent. Still, Ryuunosuke had faith. His belief that he could reach Rinne somehow was based only on his naive trust in her.

"You don't deserve to die, Rinne! A person like you shouldn't be put to death! You're strong, beautiful, and lovely! A bit silly sometimes, but that only adds to your charm! You can be overbearing, but at the same time, you're nervous in social situations! You can be arrogant and proud, but you'll do everything for those you care about! This is the person I know you as!"

They'd only been together briefly, but already, Ryuunosuke couldn't imagine the world without Rinne.

"I swear…"

Ryuunosuke did other people's work for them, saved the bullied from their bullies, took anemic students to the nurse's office, and helped people carry heavy bags. To him, saving a life or saving the world was the same kind of a good deed. Not to say he didn't attach much value to the world or human lives, but in his eyes, helping was always important, whether it was simply everyday help, or something as extraordinary as rescuing a person or saving the entire world from destruction. It was just in his nature.

That voice he knew but didn't, the scene he'd never seen before but felt was all too familiar, his sense of duty—he became convinced everything was connected, and part of the destiny that had led him up to that day.

"I'm going to…," he shouted, and the dragon reached toward him.

◆

She loved him.

*   *   *

The girl was truly in love with the boy, and that's why her devil had to kill him. It would kill him because of love, because of the girl's bond with him. The boy's existence was very unfortunate from the devil's point of view.

Dying would bring the boy salvation, so it would be for the best anyway; that much was clear.

The devil and the girl were two sides of the same coin. Killing the boy would also be the best for the girl.

She didn't want to kill him. She loved him; she adored him.

She loved his eyes. So he had to die. She loved his hands. So he had to die. She loved his voice. So he had to die. She loved his cooking. So he had to die. She loved how kind he was to everyone. So he had to die. She loved him for saving her. So he had to die. She loved him for treating her with care. So he had to die. She loved his warmth, his smile, every single cell that made up his body, all of him, from the top of his head down to his toes. So he had to die. He was too good for that world.

She wanted to share her life with him.

Even his shortcomings seemed like virtues to her. She didn't know the difference between affection and all the different levels of love, but she had no doubt that she was in love with him.

He was so incredible; she loved him so much. So he had to die. He had to be set free from this twisted world. That was what she'd decided.

"That's why! I'm!"

He kept shouting at her, even though he must have known he couldn't reach her. Not with his voice, not with his hands. She couldn't respond to him anyway. She wouldn't. There'd be no miracle. The chance of her responding was exactly 0 percent. It was impossible, ridiculous to imagine. Inconceivable.

That was how mythical girls worked—going absolutely berserk made it impossible for them to engage with anyone.

The devil would kill the boy, then destroy the world. It would write the final chapter in this world's story.

Ever since the first appearance of a mythical girl in this world, never had one been saved after reaching the second phase of berserk status. There had been no precedent, and none would ever be established.

An evil force of destruction, a calamity threatening humanity, could not hope to be saved.

"Going to!"

The devil reached toward the boy, not in response to his voice, but to kill him.

"Save you!"

The boy's voice was drowned out by the cracking of his bones burning to ashes. The dragon had fired its gauntlet at him, blasting away his upper body.

"What a fool," the devil said mockingly.

It heard the crackling of a burning human body; it smelled the stench of burning hair. Nothing was left of the boy from the waist up. The open wound wasn't even bleeding, having been cauterized by the hot beam.

"Death renders everything meaningless."

The boy had no way of dodging the dragon's attack. It was impossible to survive it.

The shackles of love had been broken. Rinne's only wish had become impossible. The world was as good as dead. A miracle didn't happen. Of course it wouldn't have. And so the fate of the world had been sealed.

"What is this...?"

Something odd was going on with the mutilated remains of the boy—flames rose from the waist, scattering softly like feathers to reveal Ryuunosuke's body being remade. For a moment, the flames formed the shape of wings behind him, and then they vanished.

Ryuunosuke was alive and well.

"Even soul linking with the vampire would not give you regenerative ability this strong... It should have been impossible for you to recover..."

Ryuunosuke hadn't been saved by Mari's healing powers. The dragon and vampire factors possessed miraculous vitality, resistance, and regenerative ability, but they weren't immortal. If they lost the entire upper part of their body, they would die.

But then how could this boy still be alive? Was he immortal?

"Impossible... Impossible... Impossible! He cannot have this ability..."

There was a mythical winged creature that transcended death, that could rise from the ashes reborn. The Fourth Factor...

"..."

The boy was looking at the dragon with vacant eyes. The girl, or rather, her devil displayed an emotion other than rage for the first time.

It was fear.

"No... You had already been wed to another before the dragon..."

Light returned to the boy's eyes.

"I've come to save you, Rinne!"

For a moment, the devil was caught off guard, and Rinne's consciousness made it to the surface. She wasted no time, grabbing the boy's hand and pressing it to the Stigma on her chest.

"I grant you permission to touch me, Ryuunosuke."

It was supposed to be impossible for him to reach her, but he had.

◆

"Help as many people as you can, for the both of us."

He heard a voice but couldn't remember who it belonged to. A scene he'd never seen before flashed in his mind. As long as that voice kept whispering to him, he would continue to help others, even if it meant putting his life on the line.

He began saying his very own pledge.

"In sickness and in health, in joy and in sorrow, for richer and for poorer..."

The pledge of soul linking.

"...even if the whole world turns against us, I will always be your ally! Together, we will survive!"

"Stop..."

Ryuunosuke ignored the devil, speaking to Rinne.

"Do you vow—"

"Stop!"

"—to share your life with me?!" he shouted.

"Nooo!"

His hand was on Rinne's mark.

"I do!" Rinne replied.

"Rinne...!"

"Ryuunosuke!"

The glowing Stigma shattered. Meanwhile, the light of Ryuunosuke's ring turned into little drops, which grew into a surging wave, washing Rinne clean of her sin.

"Stop it! No, no, noooooooooo!" the devil shrieked.

Its voice, which Rinne had heard for as long as she could remember, grew quieter and quieter. Her Stigma finished dissolving, and a Sacred Sealing Ring formed around her finger. The soul linking was complete. This time, it didn't suppress the devil—it erased it from existence.

The girl and the world had been saved. The girl's dragon horns, wings, tail, and armor broke off and disappeared.

Still surrounded by speckles of light, Rinne embraced Ryuunosuke to stop him from collapsing.

"Thanks, Rinne. For coming back."

"Thank you for saving me."

She was no longer giving off fierce heat, but she felt warmth in her heart. Every day, hour, minute, and second she'd spent with Ryuunosuke made her love for him grow.

Her love for him was probably going to keep growing even stronger.

The dragon embraced her chosen human, showing him her love.

"Ow, ow, ow, ow, not so hard!" Ryuunosuke protested, laughing and hugging Rinne back.

She had so much love for him, it was probably impossible to express it in just one hug, but it would do for the time being. She'd communicate her love to him little by little over time.

"..."

Ryuunosuke had fallen silent.

"Ryuunosuke? Is something wrong?"

"..."

His eyes had rolled back. Drool was leaking out of the corner of his mouth. He'd passed out. After the stress of the fight for Rinne and the physical damage he'd regenerated from, his brain had just shut down as soon as everything seemed safe again.

"Huh?! Ryuunosuke?! Eek!"

He'd gone limp in Rinne's embrace, and she was struggling not to lose her balance.

Meanwhile, Mari awoke and got up from the ground. She saw how floppy Ryuunosuke was in Rinne's arms and panicked.

"What's going on...? You're making so much noise... It's you, lizardbrain?! Ryuunosuke?! Is... Is he dead?!"

"Wh-wh-what do we do now?"

"Why are you asking me?!"

The sun began to set over a world that didn't seem to have been so close to annihilation just minutes earlier.

Bouquet Toss from the Guillotine

"The disappearance of the Ragnarok phenomenon has been confirmed. Destruction caused by the berserk Third Factor has not been officially declared. The calamity has been stopped before escalating from stage two."

"I see. The world has escaped destruction yet again, unfortunately. Any yields from Loki?"

"The data has been submitted for analysis, but he didn't leave any materials detailing his research process that led to the creation of the Synthetic Sealing Ring. It's uncertain whether we'll be able to infer how he arrived at that invention based on the result data alone..."

"Well, that's a loss we must accept. We were collaborators, not partners. While it's deplorable that we've lost a valuable resource, he'd already been immensely useful to us. There's always a trade-off between genius and sanity. As for us, we cannot afford to sacrifice the latter. We'll have to try another approach from now on."

"And your orders regarding the Calamity Research Institute and the Order?"

"Maintain our current relationship with them. We're not at a point where we can upset that balance."

"And the Sacred Sealing Ring?"

"No changes regarding the singularity, either. The girls' march to their execution continues."

"Understood. Blessed be the spring of our new world."

"Blessed be the spring."

◆

"So the world's been saved." Ranko summed up the events, throwing Ryuunosuke a bunch of flowers. "But there won't be a fanfare or end credits. It's not over—there's a ton of boring work left to deal with the aftermath. We've got to cover up the unnatural weather phenomenon and that mountain getting blown away. There'll be brain-numbing meetings to discuss whether we'll abandon the destroyed facility. But that's all work for grown-ups. Students don't need to worry about it."

"But you're a student, too."

"Exactly. For now, at least, I can enjoy a life of leisure."

Ryuunosuke was sitting in a hospital bed, holding the flowers Ranko had brought him. She was briefing him about the events since he'd saved the world.

The room was very neat and furnished more like it was in a hotel rather than a hospital. The Calamity Research Institute must have been behind Ryuunosuke getting a VIP room at Kokonoe Hospital.

It'd been three days since the world-threatening cataclysm had been averted. After saving the world, Ryuunosuke passed out and slept for those three whole days. He had to be taken to the municipal hospital since the CRI's underground facility had been partially destroyed and not all the necessary medical equipment could be salvaged. He'd only just woken, and the first thing he saw was Ranko's face as she peered closely at him.

"You don't seem to be suffering any aftereffects. Good to see you've been pretty much left unharmed."

"Yeah, I sure am glad to be okay."

"It must be thanks to a synergy between the regenerative abilities of the dragon and vampire factors, I suppose… Well, there's not a scratch on you. Linking with multiple mythical girls seems to have no adverse effect."

"Except memory loss, maybe? I remember everything up to getting close to Rinne, but not really what happened after that... Oh, and what about you? The research facility was badly damaged, wasn't it? Did you not get hurt?"

"No, I was fine. See, I'm a picture of health. Funny, though—I also have trouble remembering the events from that day, which is going to make writing a report hella difficult. I woke up in a hospital bed, like you."

"At least everything ended well, somehow. It really was a miracle, huh?"

Ranko shook her head.

"No, it wasn't. It wasn't a miracle that saved the world."

"No...?"

"I have pieced it together after reviewing camera footage from the facility. It revealed the decisive factor that led to the fortunate saving of the world."

"And that is...?"

"Simply put, love."

"Love?" Ryuunosuke frowned. "That sounds really cheesy...and unscientific? I don't see how an electrochemical state of the brain played a part."

"Don't make it sound sciency, that's *my* job. Anyway, I'm not making this up. Emotional states are integral to the workings of Sacred Sealing Rings and mythical girl powers. Every mythical girl researcher would agree that emotions have a significant effect on the soul. Rinne's love for you is so strong that even in her berserk state, her soul called out to yours, enabling it to respond to your ring and win against her devil. That's my analysis, anyhow."

"So grit prevailed."

"You could say that. Strong will was definitely essential on both sides. Rinne's undying love for you and your dogged perseverance made it happen. You kept reaching toward her, calling to her. So it was not a miracle, but the result of the strong feelings you had for each other. The feelings of—"

"I get it, love."

Ranko nodded.

"On a different topic, was everyone else at the facility okay?"

"Yes. Thankfully, everyone safely evacuated when the alarm sounded."

"Good to hear! Um, one more thing… You had Rinne move in with me to keep her stable, but in the end, she did go berserk. The CRI isn't thinking about…executing us both for that failure, is it?"

"No, of course not."

Ranko laughed.

"Nobody involved in the Dragon Babysitter Project is going to face any repercussions. The incident was due to the higher-ups and our internal security not taking any action to find spies in our organization despite my repeated warnings. The council can't blame us for Rinne going berserk or for any damage she caused."

Ryuunosuke was very relieved to hear that.

"Furthermore, the project has been granted an extension since you've proven the effectiveness of the ring. And the good news doesn't end there."

"What more have you got?"

"I've confirmed that Heimdall, the End-Bringer Factor, has been removed from Rinne's astral plane."

"Which means…?"

"Her devil's gone for good."

"Cool…?"

"It means she's not at risk of going berserk ever again. She's not an ordinary girl now, since her mythical factor remains, but she's been freed from the evil part."

"Oh, wow… That's amazing…"

Ryuunosuke exhaled deeply, happy and at ease.

"President, I think I found a new calling."

"Oh?"

"I want to erase all the mythical girls' devils so that they can live normal lives."

"What a coincidence... That's my calling, too."

Ranko gave Ryuunosuke a strange look that he wasn't sure how to interpret.

"By the way, Dazai boy..."

"Yes?"

For some reason, Ranko's usual smugness was gone, and she was blushing, looking uneasy.

"...I'm...tremendously grateful to you for what you'd done, and I'm also really sorry. I just...really owe it to you, for everything. I'm the one responsible for getting you involved in the first place."

"Hey now, it's cool. I'm always happy to help a friend."

"You've made a monumental contribution to the CRI. I'm sure you'll get compensated handsomely."

"Haven't even thought about it. That'll be nice."

"But aside from that, I'd also like to...give you something as thanks from me personally."

"Well, I won't say no to presents!"

"A-are you sure? Well, don't complain later. Here it is..."

Ranko swiftly lifted his chin with her finger and pressed her lips to his. For a while, the room was silent except for the ticking of the clock on the bedside table. After some time, and Ryuunosuke had no idea how long it had been, Ranko broke the kiss.

"You've really done well." She praised him, her face flushed. "To fulfill your wish, you must not die. Keep giving it your all. Well, that's everything I wanted to say."

Even her ears had turned red. Without waiting for his reply, she hurried out of the room, looking embarrassed.

Ryuunosuke's mind had gone blank. He'd only just woken up in the hospital, and suddenly, he was getting kissed by Ranko.

"...Huh?"

He looked at his hand, feeling an odd sensation. On his ring finger was a ring of light.

AFTERWORD

If you're new to my fiction, nice to meet you! And if you've read something by me before, nice seeing you again! I'm Daigo Murasaki, the author of this book.

Guillotine Bride is a brand-new novel I've written. The title has kind of brutal vibes, but it's a fast-paced, lively story with a bunch of girls as central characters. I hope you like it!

I'm guessing some of you want to ask me, what the heck is going on with *Demon Lord 2099*? Please rest assured I'm working on the next volume. It'll be out someday!

I started keeping a diary recently. When I was a student, I had an online diary for a while. I just like writing, stories, diaries, anything except afterwords since I don't know what to write. So instead, here's a recent excerpt from my diary.

XX/YY Dentist, dentist, dentist. Pain, pain, pain.
BB/CC I woke up. Can't remember what I dreamed about.

I don't think I'll keep up writing this diary much longer.
Moving on...

I'd like to give my thanks to Kayahara for the lovely and beautiful illustrations. I love each and every one of them, but most of all—the sleepy-looking student council president. Heh-heh!

Next, thank you to my editor! Let's go out for a meal again sometime.

Finally, thanks to all my readers! I'm so glad you decided to spend your time reading my book. I think about that sort of thing often. You do me a great honor.

Honestly, I wish we didn't have to do this whole formal afterword. A few "Thanks! Loved the story!" comments from you would make my day.

Anyhow! Talk to you later, sometime!

Daigo Murasaki